The Duke's Headstrong Woman: True Love In London

Virginia Vice

CONTENTS

CHAPTER ONE

From the sparkling coasts of India's shores to the rough frontier of Canada; along the steamy coasts of British Africa and the harsh Australian climes, Lady Nadia Havenshire had ventured across and beyond the scope of the empire her father considered himself a proud part of. She'd shared dinner with company men in the islands near Siam and she'd fanned herself in the steaming sands of the Near East.

Now life back in dreary northern England seemed positively dull - though not simply for the change of weather, but that figured quite a bit into her frame of mind no doubt. Her father, the Duke of Emerys, had sent for Lady Havenshire - and though she had enjoyed life outside the prison of waistcoats and dresses and dinner parties and 'courting' and old Lady Henrietta's gossip, Nadia's father had always treated her well and had loved her dearly; or, at least, he'd treated her as well as a father could treat a daughter when straitjacketed by the expectations of society built against daughters. She loved her father, but that silent resentment could never be undone - even, or perhaps especially considering, all she'd learned while traveling the world.

Lady Nadia had seen women across, and even outside, her father's beloved British Empire - of course, the social constants remained the same; women were mothers, women were daughters; women fed the family and women kept the home, and this was no different from the expectations of many women in the world from which Nadia had come. Things were not always the same, though, much to her surprise. In the ports along the coasts of the fledgling America, Nadia had even seen women drinking and dancing with sailors! In Africa, she'd seen local women hunting; fighting, protecting their kin, with status the same as their beloved brothers and husbands. The thought fascinated her, and she'd even indulged in the thought of abandoning the craggy, rain-spattered forests of northern England for a life free of expectations, as a woman indulging in the freedom so often afforded English men.

Instead, she sat in a carriage rolling across cobblestones, the clop-clop of horse hooves her only comfort, the whistle of her driver faint and dull, like a cudgel banging against the base of her skull. She rubbed her temples; the trip across the sea hadn't been comfortable, as she'd been forced to book passage at the last minute on any ship that would take her, and wound up amid rowdy sailors amid a creaking wooden frame tossed by rough waves, water creeping and seeping through every hole and loose crease and every rotted beam on the timber-woven frame. The to-and-fro left her back sore and her head pounding in faint ache, and on the long trip from the ports along the roads to northern England she'd spent two days bouncing and bobbing gently, until the rhythm had made her back numb.

She expected about the same level of comfort when she attempted to ease back in to her 'old' way of life. She didn't know that she'd be able to go back to that ever again - not with the knowledge she'd gained abroad. She'd met teachers, strong women and strong men who saw her and wanted to see her actualized, as they termed it. One of women who'd accompanied her on her trip to Africa had taught her a woman's place is wherever she wishes; the headmaster of a boarding school had taught her arithmetic, language, and literature, and had commented that Lady Nadia took to education as a fish to the English Channel. More than anything, Lady Havenshire had learned her worth while sailing the seas and venturing into lands few had ever seen. And when a woman with heart and spirit like Lady Nadia Havenshire learns she has worth to the world, the idea of subjugating that worth in a society controlled by men feels less and less appealing with each clopping hoof-step taken along the rural roads towards towering manses and cloaking forests.

When the carriage carried Nadia past the crumbled stone wall along the roadside, and she began to recognize the old weathered posts holding dead lanterns that swayed with passing breezes, she knew she'd arrived at the fringed edges of the Duchy of Emerys, the leaf-choked land of green and plenty she'd left behind years ago. Now turning twenty, Nadia's gut sank as she thought on precisely what she'd be expected to do with her waning youth. To the world in northern England, many women her age had already found men to marry; dukes to court them and to control their lives, making decisions for the young women so that they'd never need to make any themselves. The very idea of a man with a title crossing the threshold of Havenshire Manor to seek her life as his to control made her wretch, and not simply because she'd seen that women could do as they wish in other parts of the world. The whole idea had always felt... wrong, to her, even as a child; perhaps that had been the reason that, upon reaching her seventeenth birthday, Lady Nadia had chosen to venture past the gates of her family's manse in the first place. She'd seen the way her friends' lives had unfolded - a childhood playmate, the Lady Emily of Staffords, had been betrothed to a man since the day she'd turned sixteen. She had not been the only one - and in spite of her father's insistences, Nadia refused to go to the debutante balls and lavish parties that her friends had wrapped themselves up so readily in. The very thought of marrying a man she'd scarcely even met, so that he could take her land and her name and title and demand of her how she would dress and talk and walk, and even what thoughts she could think... none of that lifestyle had appealed to her, even in her youth. Her father had always called her a 'willful, blythe young spirit.' She'd never known what it meant, but after her time among beggars and teachers and kings in foreign lands, perhaps she'd begun to see just what he had seen in her.

"We'll be coming up on the gates soon, m'lady," Egan commented. Her father had had the courtesy of sending a man Nadia knew and could trust; Egan, an aging, rotund laugh of a man with stringy, graying hair and a bushy beard, had gained quite a bit of weight since Nadia had last seen him, though it only added to the boisterous, loud and jolly chauffeur she had known since her youth. He hummed away, which while it would normally give her a sense of peace of mind, instead only created an unnerving reminder of what she was returning to.

"You've hummed the same tunes for twenty years, Egan," she commented wryly, her head pulsing and her heart pumping; the sound reminded her of home, and being reminded of home didn't quite have the comforting cheeriness it held for many others. To her home was a doomed existence she had no interest in. "Haven't you learned any new tunes since I've been out of England?"

"Your father was always right about you, since you were a little thing, Lady Nadia," Egan chortled, glancing through the window in the wall separating the damp, cool air of England from the cramped confines of the rather spartan carriage Nadia's father had sent to fetch her. "A willful firebrand of a daughter, he said you'd grow up to be."

"And I'm presuming your implication is that I grew up to be willful? Is a woman willful for wanting to hear a different tune, Egan?" Nadia responded with a grin. She had no shame in that title, though she knew it would be spoken scathingly in the whispers of crass bachelors discussing available brides with prestigious titles.

"I only know that when your father hired me he admonished me, asking me to hum a few tunes for him to break the silence. And now, with as much conviction as he had, you want me to stop. You're certainly his daughter," Egan said with a nod.

"I didn't say stop. Just a different tune, is all," Nadia protested.

"The classics never change," Egan joked. Concern crossed Lady Nadia's face; she reasoned that perhaps she could divine some of the details of this rather sudden visit of hers from Egan, who had always been one of her father's loyal and trusted servants. Before he began to hum again, she interjected quietly.

"Egan, have you any idea why my father's sent for me? I had not forgotten about him, or about the family estate, but I simply had been enjoying my time abroad, learning of the way of things. Certainly not something he could fault me for, yes?" she asked, guarded, fearing that perhaps something had angered her father and that on her return she would be subject to his wrath.

"Oh, no, I don't think your father considered you estranged or anysuch, m'lady, at least not by the manner in which he spoke of you.

Not a fiber in him has lost love for his only child, I assure you, Nadia,"
Egan laughed. That did little to assuage her fears, though. Lady Nadia
could handle an argument with her father - and if nothing so simple
faced her when the carriage climbed the hill upon which Havenshire
Manor sat, fear of the unknown struck her instead.

"Then... what could have troubled him, do you think?" Lady Nadia
asked innocently. Egan hesitated; she could feel a tension in him, as his
eyes kept to the broad and empty road; the silence mired her in dread.

"Begging your pardon, m'lady, but I think it... best, for Lord
Havenshire to explain the situation to you himself. I'm but a simple
driver, after all," Egan commented, and she knew what that particular
choice of words meant; he was playing ignorant, perhaps at the direct
request of her father. Frustrated and quietly frightened, Nadia's breath
rattled as she exhaled deeply.

"Certainly, he wouldn't be cross with you for giving a single hint of
a detail, Egan?" Nadia whispered, closing conspiratorially towards the
window near Egan's ear. She could see his features - vexed, perhaps by
his loyalty to her father, but most certainly vexed just the same with a
deep-seated worry of his own.

"You're a woman who's come of age, m'lady, and your father
has... concerns, quite reasonable concerns, as to the disposition of the
family estate. These are, of course, concerns common to every man and
woman of station, m'lady, and so you... need not worry too greatly,
yes?" Egan tempered rather grave matters of speech with a comforting
tone and a toothy grin, but Nadia could tell that whatever had
happened troubled trusty Egan just as deeply as it troubled her father.
Nadia saw no need to press; she knew Egan would reveal little else.

With worry on her brow Lady Nadia reclined across the carriage's padded bench, watching the countryside roll by. She recognized the landmarks; the crumbled statue, an old guardhouse situated along a long-rotted wooden wall. Much of the manse appeared frozen in time; her father had little interest in the stodgy cobbled-together structures that had once littered the grounds, preferring the bright and dominant architecture of the new designers from London, with windows and white paints and swirling facades lit by the glow of the sun. Still, something cast a long shadow over the rest of the trip - and not just her own pained memories of men slighting her or the controlled society she had now chained herself to once more, the manacles tightening further and further with each step taken closer to the manse.

"We'll be scaling the hill soon, m'lady," Egan said, rather dour; the remainder of the trip came in silence. No more humming, no more curious questions; no laughs or boasts of joy. Whatever had driven this reunion weighed heavily on the both of them.

CHAPTER TWO

"Quite a ride, eh, m'lady?" Egan asked, once more wearing his usual manner of joyful grin, though it felt far more manufactured now than it had been in years past, as if he hid something beneath the mask of mirth. Lady Havenshire stepped out of the carriage, the breathtaking size of the manor reminding her starkly of how small the world here was, where a wealthy duke's manor, garden, and the bounteous lands beyond dwarfed so much of the surroundings. The sun setting as evening began to creep in, Lady Nadia yawned, holding her gloved fingers to her lips out of courtesy. The windows, an entire gleaming array of them, spat back her reflection as the sun shone brightly; dressed in her simplest dress, a lacy affair of golden-yellow with a laced bodice of brilliant pearly white, her hair fell in curled, vibrant fiery-auburn coils along her dainty shoulders. Though she had a reputation as trouble among the local nobles, she didn't quite have the imposing stature of the firebrand they certainly all imagined - a petite woman, of only five feet tall and a thin, lithe figure, that small personage hid a vibrant mind and independent personality.

"One never quite realizes how large the estate is, until spending so much time away, Egan," she commented in a quiet tone. Standing tall and broad, with rows upon rows of windows and white pillars and archways, the mansion reminded her of the pictures of crumbling temples of classical antiquity, rebuilt to soar as they had in their prime, and glowing with a glorious marbled sheen. Egan offered his hand to escort her through the garden pathway and to the manor's front door; wrought-iron trellises overgrown with vibrant white-tipped ivy leaves lined the entrance to the mansion, beds of sprouting flowers nestled at their metal feet.

"Nelson has done quite well keeping the gardens as alive as I remembered," Lady Nadia observed.

"You won't let me escort you into the manor, m'lady?" Egan said with a frown, his hand still outstretched as the redheaded woman passed him by. With a playfully chiding look she turned to the aging chauffeur, her arms crossed atop her chest.

"You expect a willful firebrand like myself to take an offer, just because you're a man?" she joked. "Would my father have accepted such a request, had he been a woman?"

"I think he would have, if only to make a tired old man happy for a few moments," Egan said with facetious sadness. Lady Havenshire sighed, smiled, and finally took Egan's hand, its surface hardened like worked leather after years of laboring and handling rough, hempen ropes.

"Is this making the tired old man happy?" Lady Nadia joked, as the two of them walked to the manor's front door. Emotions overcame the aging driver, a longtime friend of the family; Nadia couldn't remember a time when Egan hadn't seen to her father and mother, before she passed. He looked away, sullen, and concern crept into Nadia's features.

"Very happy, just like when you were a girl," Egan said, his hand shaking.

"Is something wrong, Egan?" Nadia asked as they reached the door, noticing the portly porter had begun to try to hide tears forming at the edges of his eyes.

"M'lady, it's your father," he confessed, his voice wobbling. "He's called you back here for a very... very important, grave matter."

"Egan, please, if this is troubling you so deeply..." Nadia implored, her own breaths shaky and unsure.

"It's... it's not my business to say, m'lady. Your father is... is waiting for you," he confessed, composing himself and wiping away tears, his eyes reddened, his head held high. He rapped loudly on the manor door, and Nadia realized that something serious had so abruptly called her away from the world and back to her home. She had never in her life seen joyful Egan so despairing as that moment; it was a despair she, too, saw in the eyes of Ms. Mulwray, an elderly woman who had served as majordomo of the house staff since before Nadia was born, when the woman answered the door. She smiled, though it felt forced, and instead of curtsies and other such performative gestures, Ms. Mulwray caught the melancholy in Egan's expression and instead embraced Nadia deeply.

In that moment Nadia knew something very serious had happened. Ms. Mulwray could be quite charming, and had always looked out for the young Nadia as she grew, but Nadia remembered her as strict; as no-nonsense. Nadia could never have imagined returning home from an exploration of the world, and of herself - an exploration Ms. Mulwray had had serious misgivings about Nadia undertaking - and being greeted with a comforting hug.

"We're all sorry to have to see you again in circumstances so grave, m'lady Nadia," Ms. Mulwray cooed in that soothing fashion she had a knack for; the soothing coo she'd heard when Nadia had skinned her knee exploring as a child. Nadia blinked, swallowing hard.

"G... grave circumstances?" Nadia asked, her heart sinking. She searched the foyer for her father, and suddenly realized that he had not gotten up and come to the door to greet her - something she had expected, after being gone for so long. It felt... wrong. Ms. Mulwray glanced with widened eyes at Egan, who cleared his throat weakly.

"You haven't spoken to her about... about the nature of the visit, Egan? I quite figured you would've already had this conversation," Ms. Mulwray announced.

"I thought it best for her to... hear, from her father, the nature of the issues facing the estate, Ms. Mulwray. Beggin' your pardon," Egan bowed his head.

"Yes, per... haps, perhaps you're onto something, Egan. Perhaps she ought to see her father," Ms. Mulwray sighed; she seemed a woman broken, not the unflinching and proud servant Nadia had known all her youth. The majordomo took Lady Nadia's hand and led her through the foyer, its vaulted ceiling and ornate oak reliefs spotless and gleaming with polish. Atop the stairs, their carpets plush and springy as she remembered, her heart began to fill with a dread that only worsened the further down the second-floor hallway Ms. Mulwray led her.

"We've quite... missed you, in your time away. Especially your father," Ms. Mulwray said, her voice cracking, the majordomo clearly as startled by... something, as Egan had been. "How have you fared? Your letters, sparse as they were," Ms. Mulwray commented with mild bitterness, "told of some rather surprising and unusual ideas and encounters."

"I've missed... father, myself. My time out was... quite

enlightening," Nadia said, distracted by her muddied thoughts.

"Please don't speak of any of that... confusing, startling nonsense you've learned of abroad with your father," Ms. Mulwray stated starkly and plainly. Nadia sighed, remembering quite well the admonitions so common from Ms. Mulwray, who chastised Nadia regularly in her youth about how women were supposed to act. "You're... liable to hurt him, to give him a terrible heart attack and just kill your loving father," Ms. Mulwray added, her voice increasingly addled with pain and sadness. Finally, the majordomo's eyes filled with tears as she chided Lady Nadia, who shook, realizing it was something more that drove Ms. Mulwray's sharp criticisms.

"Ms. Mulwray, what's wrong with my father?" Nadia asked plainly. Ms. Mulwray shook her head, wiping away tears; trying to face whatever waited on the other side of the door they now stood before with strength.

"He's a fragile man, Lady Nadia. Please, take that into your heart, and listen to him," Ms. Mulwray pleaded, as she threw the door open, wearing the same mask of a smile that Egan had put on. "M'lord, I present the lovely Lady Nadia, returning from travels to exotic lands to see her father," Ms. Mulwray exclaimed. Nadia took a step in to her father's bedchambers - the curtains pulled shut, with only the faint flicker of lit candelabras and hung lanterns to light the dark room, its lavish furniture and accoutrements cloaked away from dust with heavy sheets. Nadia's vision took a moment to adjust, and she wondered just why the curtains had been drawn shut; why her father lay in bed so early in the eve. Confused, Nadia stepped in, and the strong scent of stale herbs and incense immediately struck her nose.

"My daughter! Nadia--" Lord Havenshire could scarcely finish a sentence before a hoarse cough gripped his throat and squeezed deep, wheezing, painful-sounding noises from his chest. Nadia recoiled; she may have spent years away from the family estate, but she had not forgotten the tenor of her father's voice - proud, full, confident, and always mirthful, even when life felt its bleakest. What had been the voice of true Lord had somehow been reduced to a ghastly, strained whisper; the closer Nadia drew to the bed, the more of her stricken father she began to see.

"I've missed you dearly, Nadia," he added, another ashen cough thick in his throat. Though the low light of the candles obscured the finer details, she could see her father - weak, his once-robust chest and shoulders shriveled; his body withered as a dried-out corn husk. Nadia's features fell, her voice quivering; her father's head had been shaved, his eyes sunken, his skin pale, sweat beading at his brow. Her lips gaping in pained shock, Nadia took a deep breath and gathered herself up.

"F... father, I've... I've missed you, too," she said, avoiding the topic of the painful, obvious issues that had befallen her father and chained him so weak and fragile to the bed.

"Is the manor what you remember of it? I've tried to have Ms. Mulwray, lovely woman she is, keep it up, just the way it had been," he smiled, or tried to smile, as best his shrunken face would let him.

"Yes, it's... it's lovely," Nadia responded absentmindedly. She fought the urge to gawk, to see what possibly could've befallen her father, but she found her eyes wandering nevertheless.

"I certainly hope our family fortune paid off. Did you learn a lot? What did you see, out there in the world past the manor?" he asked, and she could hear even through the hoarse whistling the coy playfulness in his tone.

"Wild ideas, father, about the world, and about life," she chuckled; she could feel Ms. Mulwray's eyes burning through her from the doorway. "Women with their own families, women teaching, women as hunters, women as equals... such pernicious ideas," Nadia joked.

"Women hunting? Come now, is that truly what you want to do? Lady Havenshire, a gameskeep?" her father laughed.

"Not a job for me, though I think a woman as a hunter, and a leader, is a curious, and useful, thought," Nadia smiled.

"I suppose that quite starkly brings into focus what I obviously need to address. Nadia, my daughter," her father sighed, and she felt her breaths wobble, nervous and weak. "I'm... certain, you can see, you're a smart young woman, as smart as ever have there been in all of England, my darling. You've no doubt already seen something awry in the household. The doctors haven't a clue of what's afflicting my head, but it's worsened and worsened until... well," he exhaled gravely. "There are matters that need tending to before... this situation worsens."

"Worsens? Father..." Nadia's voice trailed away, shaking, a tear stinging the corner of her eyes. "What's... what's happened to you?" she finally asked flatly.

"I can feel myself at the end of this journey, Nadia, but I need to get into order the matters of my household - and my daughter - after death takes me," her father stated bluntly. She swallowed, fighting away tears, her fists tightened.

"Death? Certainly... you're exaggerating, father," Nadia stated with a muted hopefulness in her tone.

"I'm not certain, darling girl, we can never be. But the taste in my mouth and the pain in my head, as every expert in England comes to my bedside, have brought into stark importance the necessity of pressing into you the importance of your inheritance, Nadia."

"My inheritance?" she asked weakly. She had an inkling of what the inheritance meant, but denial took her mind more than any other thought. She couldn't dare think of parting with her father... not so early into her adult life. "Father, we only need worry about your health."

"Your inheritance... Nadia," he said with a sigh. "I'm certain you're not terribly amenable to this idea. But the way our world works, is the way it works, and as smart and free and capable a woman as I've watch you grow in to... there are things not even you can change, my darling." Nadia fought away the tears, unsuccessfully, as they ran across her cheeks in stuttering streams. "I have to be certain of our family's future... of your future, my daughter."

"Father, you know me capable of taking care of the estate," Nadia chimed. "You know you can trust myself and the servants to--"

"I have full faith in you, my daughter," the stricken lord coughed hoarsely. "That's... not what concerns me. You know the world that you live in. And you know that to inherit the estate and to carry on the family legacy... you need to be married, Nadia," he added gravely. "I'm old, and hurting. I'm dying, Nadia. I need to know that you'll be safe. That our name, our manor - that it will live past me."

"Father..." Nadia's voice trailed, her thoughts clashing in scattered directions. Indignant was she at the fabric of society that forced this onto her; the world where men controlled wealth, men controlled lands; men controlled names. It opposed everything she had learned, everything she had thought whifle traveling the world; more than anything, it made no sense. "I'm the person most capable-- I know this land, our people, our name..."

"I understand your trepidation, my dear, but... I can't bear to see my only daughter stand alone, unwed, should I die," her father said. A coughing flurry filled the air as he held his hand over his mouth; it seemed almost skeletal, skin stretched tight against each finger. "There are fine men, Nadia, across all of England, you know... fine men more than deserving of your attention," he tried to convince her. Nadia looked away; sighed. She could scarcely bear to see her father so weak and wracked with these concerns, but she hated the thought of giving her life away to be another trophy on some sleazy 'gentleman's' shelf.

"Father, I'll..." Nadia closed her eyes. She hated lying. "I haven't returned from my travels simply to settle in to an existence that goes against who I am. On my way back here, I spoke with Egan, and he reminisced on you in your younger days, commenting on how strong-willed you had been. If you had been a woman, as I am... do you think you would rejoice in the thought of consigning yourself to subordination? To a life as a symbol, and not as a person, father?..." a feeling of guilt crept into her knotted stomach; she hated to bring such philosophy to her clearly ailing father, but she knew what his answer would be - if he answered honestly, at least.

"Please... consider, for my own sake, Nadia," he implored. She swallowed, looked away. Her pride bristling, her emotions on a wire, she at least needed to put his heart at ease... even if hers was afire.

"I'm sorry, father," she exhaled deeply, spinning away on her heels and, eyes closed and tears on her cheeks, hastily retreated into the hall.

CHAPTER THREE

"M'lord Beckham, your dinner's about to be served," the chipper old man in the white waistcoat announced, peering quizzically into the darkened study of his master, lit only by the dying crackle of a sooty fireplace. No response came at first; its walls arrayed with shelves upon shelves of books and scholarly work, with a grand armchair facing the fireplace, the butler strode through the doorway, bowing his head as he came to see his master, shrouded in shadow, glinting, fiery embers reflected in his striking, deep green eyes; his garb colored in tones of earth and midnight, he cupped his chin in his hand, focused deeply in a myriad of contentious thoughts; his frame tall and strong, he nonetheless seemed a ghost of a man, vexed by a thousand scattered worldly concerns.

"M'lord," the voice repeated, quieter this time. The man in the chair appeared unmoved; he watched the flames lick and and listened to the cool crackle of searing embers, pondering a great many, endless things. Lord Marshall Beckham, the Duke of Berrewithe, had a lot to think about - and not just the nature of the world and the title that bore down on his shoulders.

He thought, far too often, about her. About the woman he had loved - about the woman he had lost. And he thought about what he had done to lose her. He thought about his endless failures; about what was expected of a true gentleman of his era. And how he'd failed to live up to every expectation with her. With the woman who still haunted his dreams - Anna.

"M'lord... Ms. Cauthfield has prepared your favorite meal for tonight. It's taken her all too to properly braise the beef," the butler implored, his voice quiet, almost conspiratorial. "She'd be quite cross should you choose to spend your eve alone in the study once more."

"I'll attend to the emotional needs of Ms. Cauthfield in time, James," the man draped across his darkened throne boomed, his voice resounding; his voice deep, powerful, and almost haunting in its own way, with a tint of broken at its tips. The butler sighed, peering into the fire with his master, as if seeking the sight of whatever broken memories and disturbed thoughts had brought him to this point in the first place.

"Have you been thinking again on the affair at Delshire Moors, Lord Beckham?" the butler asked, as if he already knew the answer.

"I'll not need to hear your lecture on the matter again, James," Lord Beckham groaned wearily, hoping to avoid a conversation his servants had offered him countless times since he left that dark place - alone, unwed, in a carriage of black, with rain raging across the hills, with the lord convinced he'd never find a heart to love him again.

"It's not a lecture Ms. Cauthfield and I offer, simply concern, m'lord. The both of us have served the family for more than a generation. We grew up with you, m'lord," the butler confesses, emotion sneaking into a voice tailored meticulously to appear blase and professional.

"My concern, is for why the headmistress of my house staff is in the kitchen, and not my cook," the vexed lord responded, clasping his hands in his lap idly. The thoughts wouldn't rush away - he heard the patter of the rain; he saw the flowered wedding bouquet he'd offered his dearest love, so long ago, trampled under the wheel of a carriage. He saw the letter she'd left him. The house staff had called her callous; cruel. He knew that it had been his own fault - for failing to live up to what he knew was expected of him. He'd never make the proper gentleman. Anna knew that. And now he'd spent night after night after night, rethinking all that he'd done - retracing every step, to see just where he'd failed. Why he'd lost himself, and why he'd never earn a woman's love again.

"No one makes the honey-braised loins just the way you like, except for her, m'lord," James insisted meekly. "Ms. Roth makes excellent stews and foods, of course. But no one does your favorites like Ms. Cauthfield."

"Is this what we hope to do to lift the veil cast across the estate, James? Braised loins and memories of childhood?" Lord Beckham lamented with a sigh.

"I know it's not quite my place to offer an opinion, m'lord, but... well, you know how Ms. Cauthfield and I felt about the... issue, at the Moors. You're a better man that that, m'lord. You're a better man than--"

"Anna. You can say her name, Mr. Malboro. Anna. There's no mystery as to what you speak of, when the topic of the situation at the moors crosses your lips. It's quite a frustrating euphemism," Lord Beckham intoned - not so much harsh, as miserable; crooning. "Your opinion is noted, though, as it has been many times over the years since I last... spoke, with Anna," he added, his heart wilting briefly.

"Then... m'lord Beckham, perhaps it would behoove you to note that you've given yourself far too much pain and regret for something

27

quite beyond your fault. If..." James held back the full brunt of his emotional tumult, only to earn to the faint glare of his master. He backed down, knowing cross words on the legacy of Lord Beckham's lost love would do little to deter the gloomy disposition of the man.

"I suppose it's time to listen to Lady Cauthfield's weekly haranguing of my self-reflection, then?" Lord Beckham asked stormily, lifting himself from the armchair and proceeding past his butler. Lord Beckham could recognize James's concerns - and he knew the old man had only the lord's best interests in his mind. But, he thought as he proceeded into the grand and sprawling hall on the third floor of Berrewithe Manor, neither well-intentioned James nor sprightly old Ms. Cauthfield would ever understand what it meant to be a man who could never again deserve the love of a beautiful woman. Neither could they know the sensation of failing at your life's duty - to make a woman happy, in the way only a gentleman could.

As his footsteps echoed through the shadowy stairwell, lush paneled stairs and walls gleaming in faint candlelight, he heard a storm rumble just beyond a wall of glass panes, elegant red-black curtains draped across the towering window at the second-floor landing. Lightning flashed just long enough for streaking of electric white-blue to illuminate his features; sullen, and tinted with the warmth of growing age, yet so deep; so entrancing, with a masculine cut to his jaw and a wild freedom to his dark hair. He gazed upon his visage, reflected in the lightning crackling through the windows; it would never satisfy him. A virile bed of stubble crested along his chin; something quite ghastly to see festering on the face of one who ought to be a proper gentleman.

The dining room doors swung open and Lord Beckham entered

silently, the scent of fresh rain falling replaced by the thick scent and sizzle of stringy beef loins braised slow in pots with honey, stock, and spices. A recipe Lord Beckham had loved since his childhood, he knew that Ms. Cauthfield cooked it in trying times; she cooked it whenever she felt the need to placate an imperfect man. Though the scent pleased him, it brought back memories no longer idyllic, but tragic; memories viewed through the shards of a broken mirror.

"You're finally here! I've been braising this meat all day," exclaimed the elderly woman in the frumpy white linens, her voice full of exasperated mirth. All at once Lord Beckham's countenance changed; while the smell of the meat and the welcome smile of his loyal maidservant would normally seem so inviting, tonight was not a night he wished to again entertain her patronizing attempts to cure his foul mood, or to hear her speak once again on how little regard she had for the lord's lost love, Anna.

"Ms. Cauthfield, I certainly appreciate the sentiment, but I feel that perhaps tonight would be an evening best spent alone, with a simple glass of sherry to keep me company. I certainly hope you won't take offense," Lord Beckham murmured apologetically. Ms. Cauthfield sighed, deflated, shaking her head.

"M'lord, we do this because we care about you - James and I," she added, as her master turned his back to the door. "You do quite understand that, don't you? We're concerned. This spell that witch has cast upon you--"

"Ms. Cauthfield, I know in no uncertain terms how poor you happen to regard Anna, but I'll not have you speaking ill of her like that so boldly to me his evening," Lord Beckham growled. "Please. Enjoy the braised loins between the house staff - I know James has quite a love for your cooking, as well. I apologize for appearing mercurial, Ms. Cauthfield, but I simply don't have it in me tonight."

"Will you ever have it in you, m'lord?" Ms. Cauthfield asked, bedraggled. He took a long, contemplative silence to consider that before leaving the dining room.

CHAPTER FOUR

"M'lord! Look at what a wonderful day it is!"

He heard the soft scrape of curtains drawn open against steely curtain-rods; he felt the sun leap through smudged windows, glaring into his pulled-shut eyes. A beautiful day had taken off across the rolling moors, and the glower of the day's burning beams pulled him harshly from reverie; a meandering and painful dream he had too often, one that he couldn't forget; one that floated through his mind almost any time he pulled his eyes shut and closed out the sound and the light and the life of the world.

Rain pattering across a courtyard; stands of roses woven through bright-white trellises, lining a cobblestone pathway. Beautiful flowerbeds flanking rows of empty benches; the disembodied sound of a reception, a party meant just for him; for him, and for his love.

Rain darkening what should have been a day to remember for all his life... a day he thought, until then, that he was born deserving. The day he and Anna would meet.

Instead he found only soggy bouquets; eyes strained wide in surprise. Gossipy murmurs as throngs of men in their white suits and women in loose, flowing gowns woven with lacy, floral patterns stood beneath the cloistered halls lining the courtyard, grass flooded as he fell to his knees, soaked by the storm that had claimed a day he had dreamed of; the day he and she would exchange something sacred and inviolable.

He closed his eyes to shoo away the sunlight for just a few more moments, so that he might masochistically recall that day; the day that haunted dreams both waking and asleep. The day that taught him he didn't deserve love. He had always heard of her as flighty; as a 'firebrand'. She never imagined that she would so quickly turn away from his love, and he could only reason that she did so, and did it so easily, because he had never earned that love in the first place. He knew he could never earn anyone's love.

How could any woman truly ever love me?

"Chase the dreams away, m'lord, it's an exciting day to wake up to," the chipper old woman's voice chimed. He opened his eyes again to see a figure cast in the shadow of the day, wrapped in sunlight that blinded him. As his eyes adjust and the muddled patter of rain from his dream ebbed away in his ears, he sighed in desperation on seeing a woman too familiar to him standing in the light at the window.

"Ms. Cauthfield, yes, good morning," Lord Beckham groaned, rolling onto his back in the bed. Confused and perturbed, his rather grumpy tone fell upon his loyal, bright-eyed servant like a particularly unceremonious cudgel. "And for what doubtlessly pressing concern have you implored me rise from bed so early?" he asked sarcastically.

"So much impudence for your family's longest-employed servant," Ms. Cauthfield humphed as she went about picking up articles of clothing scattered about the bedroom, straightening the lord's writing desk as she passed. "I helped raise you, you know. Your mother, may she rest peacefully, found herself so often utterly baffled on what to do with you, m'lord. I think on her often," Ms. Cauthfield sniffled nostalgically. "And with how you've been these past years, m'lord, I can certainly begin to understand how at a loss she was, regarding you."

"Ms. Cauthfield, don't you think it's perhaps a bit early in the day for one of your brow-beatings?" Lord Beckham lamented, sighing as he came to sit on the edge of the bed, chasing away a long yawn.

"Would you prefer it if I perhaps waited until dinner time, instead?" Ms. Cauthfield responded with a cheery chirp, responding to his facetiousness with a rapier-strike of her own. "By then you'll be quite prepared, won't you?"

"You're fortunate to have a master as caring and as forgiving as I can be, Ms. Cauthfield," the lord grumbled; the old woman showed no amount of intimidation, knowing that the master was quite a bit of bark, but far too kind a man inside to bite.

"Besides, I have to give you your verbal switchings now, as you'll be quite tied up by dinnertime, won't you?" Ms. Cauthfield asked knowingly. Lord Beckham couldn't recall precisely what the old woman was referring to, his expression perplexed. He had not exactly developed much of a habit of inviting company to the manor for dinner... though Ms. Cauthfield often had little hesitation in arranging such dates on his behalf, the precocious old woman.

"And to whom have you extended an uncalled-for invitation to my manor for this evening, then, Ms. Cauthfield?" he asked accusingly, standing and straightening the loose silken garments clung to his strong frame, his virile, broad chest exposed by the low-cut neckline.

"I should take it with no surprise but only a consigning sigh, that you've already forgotten what happens this evening, shouldn't I?" Ms. Cauthfield exclaimed in disappointment. After another night of tossing dreams; of visions of red roses left in the rain, lovingly-cut flowers trampled beneath pounding horse hooves, he had little notion in his mind to entertain these sorts of motherly naggings, even from Ms. Cauthfield, who he gave quite a bounteous handful of leeway to.

"Ms. Cauthfield, I apologize for not having quite the vastness of memory to commit to my everyday thoughts each one of the ill-advised attempts you make to socialize me back into a world with which I have no interest of engaging," Lord Beckham dismissed, disgruntled, as he walked to the windows, the sunlight blurring his vision for a brief moment. The bright gleam of fresh, tall grass growing wild along the forested fringes of the Berrewithe Estate nearly blinded him - and with each balmy glint of morning dew that met his eyes, he recoiled as the sound of distant storms replayed that sullen day in his head, over and over again, reinforcing that he ought to stay right where he was - locked away, unworthy and unwanted, in the rotting depths of Berrewithe.

"But this particular event, with which you have so stubbornly refused to engage, is a particularly important one, one I would have quite expected you to commit to memory," Ms. Cauthfield chastised in a playful sing-song as she fastidiously collected dirtied linens from the master's bed.

"I'm certain that you've said just that about *every* particular event you've attempted to coax me in to paying attention to, Ms. Cauthfield, so once again you'll need to narrow the field for me," Lord Beckham grunted acerbically.

"By particularly important, I meant *particularly* important, m'lord," Ms. Cauthfield insisted, once again inspiring the eye-rolling ire of her master. "You certainly recall the Lord Hiram Perrywise, don't you?" she asked cheerily, placing the linens in a wicker basket she'd brought up with her. Her habit of combing over the master bedroom so attentively made Lord Beckham anxious, and she knew that quite well; Ms. Cauthfield often used just that anxiousness to coax him, as she couldn't count the number of times she'd heard him say 'I'll do whatever it is you wish, so long as you stop toying with the bedsheets.' It was the only way she could get him to agree to anything, of late.

"I recall that the Lord Hiram Perrywise is a rather insufferable man with a penchant for flaunting each and every inconsequential event in his life via numerous crowded dinner parties held at his unflatteringly gaudy estate. Is that the Lord Hiram Perrywise you're speaking of, Ms. Cauthfield?" Lord Beckham asked with a sardonic grin on his stubble-laden expression. "That one?" he repeated playfully. "Certainly one of my favorite lords in all of northern England."

"You've made a habit of judging any man unworthy of your attention, Lord Beckham," Ms. Cauthfield exclaimed bitterly, "without giving them so much as a chance at earning your respect." Something about that stung deep, like the burning bite of a gnat. Perhaps in her statement he saw a harshness reflected in his own past - he had become quite a harsh adjutant of character, but it felt fair - as he applied those same standards to himself. He had long before judged his own character as unworthy of capturing the attention of fawning aristocracy - and, perhaps most painfully and damningly, the attention of a worthy, beautiful woman. Her statement cut at his core and he turned from her, consigning his sight to the sun - upon which storm clouds had begun to encroach. No day, it seemed, could pass without the darkness of a consuming storm.

"Lord Perrywise is an obnoxious and conceited man, Ms. Cauthfield, and I'm not certain why you'd consider any manner of meeting with him to be one of special importance," Lord Beckham spoke coldly, watching as swabs of gray stretched across the dying sunlight, a distant boom of thunder rattling through the moors. He watched tiny pinpoints of people across the distant farmlands scatter towards the barns and huts dotting verdant fields of swaying grains, the storm warding off hard workers. People felt so insignificant from Lord Beckham's window, the distance between he and the world outside just as great as the oceans spanning the breadth of the world.

"Lord Perrywise is of little consequence to me, m'lord. However, you are of consequence, a great amount of consequence," Ms. Cauthfield implored, her voice a little shaky. "I've given you the speech plenty of times, m'lord. I... don't think I need to rehash the worry brewing in my breast over the self-flagellation you've endured since the day at the Moors. You can't lament that loss forever, and you have so much to give to the world, if you'll understand my meaning, m'lord," Ms. Cauthfield whispered. "I know you're a fully-grown man, a man of purpose and power. I respect who you've become, m'lord, and I'm proud to have seen you through it over all the years I've served the Beckham family. I'm ... simply, worried," Ms. Cauthfield confessed. "There's always a second breath to take of life, m'lord. I know... how you felt, about Anna Brigham, but--"

"Please, Ms. Cauthfield, don't say her name," Lord Beckham pleaded, a pained expression crossing his face. "I understand... I appreciate, your concerns for me."

"Then perhaps you'd appreciate honoring my one request. Yes, I know Lord Perrywise isn't exactly the most enrapturing of hosts, but you know the rather broad crowd that his dinner parties draw. You're bound to find at least one person interested in the matters at Berrewithe - and in you, m'lord," Ms. Cauthfield implored, taking the wicker basket up, filled to its top with soiled linens. She stood, and she waited - hoping for a response, any sort of response. His eyes set on the rolling moors, Lord Beckham's ears caught the distant roar of thunder... and he saw it; rain cascading across the far-off fields, coating rolling greens with sullen memories. His eyes closed, he saw it again; Ms. Cauthfield's voice fell to a fragile, reverberating murmur. She'd worried about him. He knew she worried... but he worried, all the same. He had a great many worries - and that world, the world of fawning words and backstabbing and lies and vexed thoughts - was one that brought him the pain he wrestled with every day; every night. Any trip beyond the walls of Berrewithe Manor could hold the chance of seeing her face - of hearing her words, and of a fresh new realization just how little he fit here, or anywhere. Just how little he was worth.

Ms. Cauthfield stood and watched his silence; she watched for a long, painful moment. With a quiet sigh, she turned to the door; she had expected his outcome. The storm rumbled louder and Ms. Cauthfield, disappointed, pressed through the threshold.

"Ms. Cauthfield," his voice suddenly rang, snapping the old woman's attention back to her master. With a deep breath, his shoulders shaking, the Duke of Berrewithe, by some miracle, had come to a rather unusual decision. "...Have my carriage prepared for this evening. I suppose I ought to see what manner of ostentatious celebration Lord Perrywise has prepared, shouldn't I?" he asked rhetorically. Ms. Cauthfield's face held back from lighting up too brightly, but she was certainly pleased to hear him.

"I'll have it arranged," she responded happily.

CHAPTER FIVE

"C'mon, m'lady, you'll try to have a little fun once we get there, eh?"

"Try is the operative word in that request, Egan," Lady Havenshire sighed, watching the trees sway. A storm had passed loudly and violently through northern England earlier in the afternoon; the leftover breezes carried dewy bulbs and moistened splashes through the air as the sun fell below the horizon, the furthest corner of the sky a fading yellow-orange as bluish moonlight began to claim the dampened moors.

"Come now, m'lady. You know as well as I how comical these dinner parties of Lord Perrywise's can be," Egan chortled; with the last few orange beams creeping over the horizon as night set in along the moors, she heard hoof clops; chatter, laughter. A glance out the window of her father's luxurious carriage brought to her the distant sight of Lord Perrywise's conspicuously ostentatious manor, with an array of similarly ridiculous-looking social climbers and hangers-on gathered in bright lights and bawdy gowns at the monumental twin-doors offering entry to any who dared expose themselves to the mess of Parisian pastels and blinding gossamer blues that Lord Perrywise seemed so gleeful to share.

"Why do you think he holds such outrageous parties, at so outrageous an estate, Egan?" Lady Havenshire queried, tapping her chin curiously, a smirk on her face.

"After he lost his wife, may she rest in peace," Egan nodded, "Lord Perrywise... well, he took quite a curious detour in terms of personality.

Perhaps the madness of loneliness clung too tight to his mind, but after that long period stuffed into his mansion with only maidservants to keep him company... suffice it to say, he's been this curious manner of fellow ever since. At least you'll have a constant source of those heady chortles you enjoy, hmm, m'lady?" Egan joked boisterously, his cheeks lit up brightly. Lady Havenshire sighed in grudging admission; one of those few things that had always brought the little Nadia of the past joy was seeing what absurd outfits and manner of speech Lord Perrywise would adopt each time he came calling on the Havenshires' doorstep.

"Such frivolities can only catch my attention and occupy me for so long, Egan," she lamented, imagining the rest of the night would consist of rather dull chatter about matters of the empire and other such nonsense that held little interest for Nadia. "Besides, you're forgetting, once that initial burst of laughter dies away, Lord Perrywise manages to make himself so insufferable."

"Well... worry not, Lady Havenshire, for I'm certain your night will be alit with entertaining conversation," Egan said, wary sarcasm thick in his voice as he spun the carriage roundabout the roadway, the light of the manor and the light chatter of partygoers filling the air.

"Have you spotted another insufferable memory of ours, Egan?" Lady Havenshire asked jokingly; Egan looked through his little window to Nadia, frowning.

"Your favorite memory, perhaps. Make certain you invoke no treasured social faux pas tonight, Lady Havenshire," Egan implored. Nadia's heart sunk, and she immediately knew which insufferable socialite would be 'entertaining' the ballroom tonight.

"You don't mean..." Lady Havenshire sighed. The door to her

carriage flung open, the high-pitch squeal of delight nearly deafened poor Nadia, who winced away from the lantern-light and the gossamer glow of the manor's illuminated windows, pouring into the small carriage like a flood.

"Lady Havenshire! Nadia, my darling, it's been so very long! Your father told me he'd sent for you, my-- I recognized his carriage and I knew he had to have sent you to see us all! M'lady, you're looking wonderful!" she spoke, her words flowing an overwhelming mile every minute. Nadia had rested in the carriage's silence, with only the rhythmic hoof-clops to bother her, for too long; to be so suddenly overwhelmed with a familiar old woman's erupting tone snapped Nadia from her dreams of freedom back to the gilded cage she'd returned to England to suffer in.

"Yes, hello, it's... good, to see you, Lady Henrietta," Nadia responded, woefully sarcastic. Either the gray-haired woman in the sky-blue gown didn't notice, or didn't mind the young woman's impudence; instead, she took Nadia's wrist and jerked her from the carriage, loudly and proudly introducing the prideful heiress to the gathered assortment of pale-white dresses, spotless breeches and curious, clean-shaven expressions.

"Everyone, everyone, please! I'd like to present to everyone the fabulous, the esteemed, world-traveled daughter of our dearest friend, Lord Havenshire, who due to ill health is unable to join us this evening - the beautiful, the alluring, my sweetest god-daughter, Lady Nadia Havenshire!" the old woman tugged Nadia forward, showing off a woman who shrunk away from all the attention. A light round of applause filled the air and Nadia forced a small smile. Lady Henrietta had been a long-time friend of her father; though, worse than anything, she had proudly held the impromptu title of rumormonger of all the northern English nobility. She proved with exceptional skill the ability to embarrass and expose immediately; Nadia had looked forward to an evening of hiding in the corner, enduring boring conversation, and sneaking through the front door as quickly as possible to flag down Egan and escape. Instead she'd now been made a feature, a highlight of the night; Lady Henrietta had even revealed the nature of her father, which was certain to attract the wandering eyes of vulture-like men looking to add another name and title on to their estates by preying on the dying wishes of her distraught father. The crowd looked expectantly on Nadia, who offered only an anxious smile, before realizing the gathered assembly expected some manner of speech. Instead, she simply curtsied, bowing her head until the chatter resumed and she felt those eyes wander away.

"Certainly, certainly, the entrance of the year! Darling, you're going to make more waves than your father ever would have expected, little Nadia," Lady Henrietta rambled, pulling Nadia by the wrist. "Now, I've spoken to your father, and he's quite excited about everything tonight, thinking it will be a wondrous evening for you--"

"You spoke to-- to my father?" Nadia inquired, bristling a little. Had this all been some ill-advised manner of setup? "What did he say?"

"Of course I spoke to him! You don't think a man as smart as your father would thrust you helplessly into the clawing arms of these gossipy, backstabbing nobles, do you?" Lady Henrietta laughed; ironic, coming from the queen of all gossip herself. "He's quite worried about you, you know, Nadia. And your inheritance," Lady Henrietta reminded, and Nadia deflated immediately. This had all just been another plan to push Nadia helplessly under the thumb of a controlling lord, to 'keep the family line' going. Full of disgust, Lady Havenshire resisted Lady Henrietta's pull, but the old socialite dragged Nadia along, the young woman's muted, gold-trimmed gray gown dragging at her feet, nearly tripping young Nadia.

"Now, I've a few ideas for lovely men I think you'd get along with quite well, Nadia," Lady Henrietta began, leading poor Nadia through the front doors and into Lord Perrywise's foyer. A grand crowd had gathered, and Nadia at once felt utterly dizzied by its size, and by the winding sounds of conversation echoing through pitched hallways. Lord Perrywise's reception, painted over the color of sky and the pink of sunset, blinded her gaze; so accustomed to the calm and dark corridors of Havenshire Manor was she that the pastel glow of lanterns reflected from cherub statues and Greek marbled carvings covered in warm yellow and white nearly knocked the breath from her. She scarcely had time to adjust to the wild colors or the dozens of men watching her, for she still had yet to contend with the old woman dragging her through the assortment of gentlemen.

"You-- you have men, you want, me, to talk to?" Nadia asked incredulously.

"Well, of course! That's what a lovely young heiress with an ailing father comes to these occasions for, is it not?" Lady Henrietta chortled obnoxiously. "Now, Lord Avery, and Lord Tybalt, they're wonderful men -- a tad on the old side, but--"

"Lady Henrietta, perhaps, did you happen to think upon whether I chose to attend simply to make my father happy, and NOT to search for

43

some suitor to sweep me away and wait for my father to die?!" Nadia protested breathlessly.

"Oh, come now! If you wish to make your father happy, you'd have your eyes peeled hawkishly in search of a man worthy of your attention! A good woman like yourself needs a man, you know," Lady Henrietta insisted as she tugged Nadia along through the crowds, the sound of spring-colored sounds from light strings plied by musicians doing little to soothe poor Nadia's pounding heart. "You know, he cares quite a lot about you, and he knows that you still have a lot to learn about life as a proper lady. That's why he's asked me to--"

"Lady Henrietta, I beg your pardon, please, but I doubt quite a great deal that my father asked you to match make for me--"

"He wanted me to look after you! So that's what I'm doing, looking after you," Lady Henrietta announced proudly. "Now, Lord Avery, he's a lovely man, a tad old, but certainly a worthy husband. He does have that... small issue, he's quite a bit... well, touchy. But that's a good thing, is it not? Oh! Or the Duke of Thrushcross, he's such a lovely old man, and he lost his poor, lovely wife, so young! He's--"

"Lady Henrietta, touchy?! You're trying to set me up with--" Nadia exclaimed in exasperation, her tolerance for the old bat reaching its limit. "I think we need to stop and discuss--"

"Oh, discussion! I love discussion. Have you any rumors to share? You visited Siam, didn't you? Such a ghastly place! But I met a man there, Lord Chester-- did you meet him?" Lady Henrietta continued unabated, and Nadia was already quite exhausted. "Lord Chester! That's a man we should meet together. Certainly, he'd love your father--"

"Love my father? But what about--"

"What about you? What about you, darling?" Lady Henrietta smiled obliviously. "Now, come, let's talk to-"

"Quiet, everyone! Quiet, for just moment!" The squirrelly, sniveling tone of Lord Perrywise gave to Nadia a much-needed reprieve from the endless stream of Lady Henrietta's banter. Nadia took a deep breath, barely able to recover from the dizzying experience; but the crowd fell silent and, perched at the top of the stairwell, the tiny, bald-headed Lord Perrywise appeared, wearing a waistcoat and jacket quite big on him, in the gaudiest combination of blinding colors Nadia could imagine - pink pastels, sky blues, and greens! His curious sense of fashion would no doubt inspire a laugh, had Nadia not been all too tired for that sort of exertion.

"I'm so-so-so very pleased, to see all of you gathered here," Lord Perrywise said, before laughing his horrifying laugh, like the melodic chirping of a bird. "I'm so wonderfully fortunate to have so many lovely friends here, willing to extend a hand of friendship, in such a friendly way," the odd man spoke in circles. Nadia had to shake the confusion from her head to make sure she'd heard his odd declarations accurately. "Now, lovely friends, dinner is prepared, BUT! I've a fun little game for us all to play. You'll find in the dining room, small plaques at each seat! You'll need to find yours - and once you find it, you'll be forced to sit among strangers! Now, friends, meet new friends!" Lord Perrywise declared; the doors to the dining room squealed on their hinges and Nadia swallowed a lump in her throat. Great. Saved from the endless irritating chatter of Lady Henrietta... only to be exposed to who knows what manner of endless, irritating chatter from strangers she'd be forced to sit next to.

"This is unexpected," Lady Henrietta frowned, before the brief moment of sadness passed and her face lit up once more. "Certainly, you'll find a lovely man to speak to -- think of your father! Now," Lady Henrietta declared, hustling with excitement towards the dining room - this was just the sort of ridiculous thing she'd enjoy, but for Nadia? She could only scoff at the thought of whatever ridiculous, old-fashioned ideas she'd be forced to endure as she yawned and pretend to need to excuse herself for the evening.

Nadia pushed her way through the crowd - so many tall people, with tall heels, long gowns; flowing jackets, laughing. She felt alone, strange, as if she'd stepped out of the real world outside of England and stepped in to a bizarre little bubble of madness - mad men, mad women, drinking wine and laughing at bad jokes together. Nadia slunk with doom in her footsteps along the long table, searching for her name; searching, searching, recognizing the names and titles of people her father had often spent time with. She recognized the names of old friends of hers; women who had once been headstrong, but who abandoned their ideas and independence when money and title and men came into their lives. Finally, at the very end of the table, she found it: LADY HAVENSHIRE. She sighed, glancing curiously at the name next to hers: LORD BECKHAM. Just perfect, she thought facetiously; a man to lecture her on the nature of marriage, or to try at her father's fortune, or both.

Nadia slipped into her chair, sinking down into the upholstery as violin music and guffaws echoed through the dining hall. She almost found a moment of uneasy peace, before a familiar voice broke into her thoughts again.

"Lord Beckham? Hmmm, isn't that the reclusive chap from Berrewithe?" Lady Henrietta asked, startling Nadia from her moment of self-reflection.

"I'm-- Lady Henrietta! Shouldn't you be finding your own name and seat?!" Nadia exclaimed in a heated whisper.

"Your father asked me to look after you, and I can't have some silly foible by old Henry Perrywise foiling your father's goodwill," Lady Henrietta declared, examining the nameplate as if it held some secret clues. "Lord Beckham... a strange fellow. I hear little of him from these events. Perhaps he'd simply rather sit up on his hill," Lady Henrietta mused.

"Or," Nadia interjected, "perhaps he simply hasn't got the time or attention span for these silly dinner parties," she responded coolly.

"Come now, darling! Every single man has his eye out for lovely ladies, and--"

"Excuse me," came a darkly-entrancing voice from behind Lady Henrietta's bird-like squawks. Nadia blinked, turning to see the source of the sound - oddly brooding, but spoken in a manner that demanded attention. Lady Henrietta froze and turned to see him - a man in a black coat, his expression dark, his face handsome but crossed with emotion. He struck Nadia silent - he was like nothing else at this ball, as out-of-place as she was, clothed in dark colors and vexed rather than pleased by the drunken follies of loud, gossiping nobles in bright-white and powder-colored coats and gowns. "I believe that spot is meant for me. No offense, m'lady," the brooding man rumbled, his voice like a soothing thunderstorm crooning quietly across the northern moors. Lady Henrietta stood in stunned silence for a moment, gathering her thoughts before a devilish grin crossed her wrinkled face.

"Certainly, m'lord, you've a wonderful little lady waiting to make conversation with you," Lady Henrietta brimmed, tossing a conspiratorial smile in Nadia's direction. Nadia cringed, the old woman admiring the new arrival, the entrancing storm of a man, as sat into the chair. Nadia got a better look at him now; tall, broad, with a deep face crested with the signs of both wisdom and strength; eyes as much a tempest as his voice, his expression so out of place somewhere like this. Nadia silently wished him to be different, so different the way she was; perhaps, she held out hope, this handsome and curious man saw the world differently, just as she did.

She could only hope. Men had little regard for women like Nadia, or their 'worldly' ideas, and she felt certain this man would prove no different. She looked away, awkwardly counting candles along the far wall. This man, Lord Beckham, didn't seem too interested in breaking the silence, either... which Nadia took to be rather interesting. Among these types it was, after all, the duty of the man to be the aggressor; such was what she came to expect.

Instead, he reclined in the chair, deep in thought on himself; so deep, it seemed, that Nadia honestly grew... a little offended. Had she not the looks of one of these other debutantes or young heiresses? Didn't she deserve his attention? Instead, since the moment he'd invited himself to sit, he'd remained silent, and she began to long to hear his powerful voice again, if only to know she was deserving of at least an inkling of his attention.

Instead, he remained silent. The chatter around them grew louder; the squealing noise of the string orchestra growing bawdier, and the life around them growing more jovial. But still Lord Beckham and Lady Havenshire remained standoffish, her arms crossed atop her chest; Lord Beckham's eyes drawn inward, looking at his own soul more than anything around them. Nadia shifted in her chair, the wood creaking beneath her; finally, the silence between them deafening and her own sense of insecurity welling up, she spoke out.

"Well, I'm rather surprised at your acquiescence, I'll say that much," Nadia bristled. "Letting the woman be the first to speak is not quite the manner I've come to expect from men of wealth in this part of the world." Lord Beckham's expression turned slowly, and when his deep, contemplative eyes fell upon her she blinked, realizing just how confrontational she had sounded.

"Pardon, m'lady. If you were expecting a wellspring of conversation, perhaps we ought to ask Lady Henrietta to come back," he spoke, words utterly deadpan. Simultaneously shocked and pleased, Nadia couldn't stop herself from erupting into a completely ugly and unladylike laugh. Lord Beckham smiled mildly. "I'm fortunate that made you laugh, else ways I'd be expecting a long and firmly-worded scolding from the old woman rather soon."

"Oh, lord, no, we'd both be getting one if she knew I'd laughed at that," Lady Havenshire whispered, chuckling. "I wasn't aware her reputation was so well-known."

"You weren't aware? Shall I call her back to make you aware? None have been so vigorous in letting all of England know that Lady Henrietta likes to talk, than Lady Henrietta herself," Lord Beckham joked. Once more Nadia let out that ugly laugh, stifling it before she embarrassed herself, though Lord Beckham's smile invited her to continue. "Please, don't be concerned on the nature of your laugh around me. This is Lord Perrywise's event, after all." Nadia blinked; she could feel her defenses falter, her heart weak and inviting for just a moment.

"Such boldness," she grinned. "You're certain you belong here? You're not some manner of rogue who slipped in unaccounted for, are you?" Nadia snarked incredulously.

"I could certainly ask the same of you, with that laugh," he teased, inviting a playful slap on the shoulder from Lady Havenshire.

"That's most uncalled for, Lord Beckham," she exaggerated his title to tease.

"Quite so, Lady Havenshire," he responded with the same sense of gravity; she expressed surprise.

"H-how did you know my name?" she intoned quizzically.

"Well, I've a secret to share," Lord Beckham's voice grew conspiratorial. "I've some great manner of otherworldly power, such that it would engender envy from the devil himself. I can see into the minds of the vulnerable, the weak-willed, and I can..." he drew closer, his voice falling to a whisper. "...read, the nameplate sat before them," he finished with a flourish, tapping on the plaque - LADY HAVENSHIRE - still set in front of Nadia. Embarrassed, she chuckled, her cheeks bright red.

"Weak-willed, huh?" she sniped back playfully. "Gullible, perhaps I'd admit, but weak-willed? Do you know who I am?"

"Of course I do," he answered without missing a beat, "You're Lady Havenshire." She blushed and tried to stifle her laughter again, her heart singing, odd yet comforting. This strange man had somehow proven himself to be different - at least, entertaining.

"That's not what I meant, Lord Beckham," she again repeated his name with that sarcastic weightiness. "You wouldn't call a woman weak-willed when she's spent the last few years traveling the world, all on her own, would you?"

"Is that what you've done? Am I meant to be impressed? I traveled across all of northern England, you know, and I'm certain that's a far greater trifle than traveling the world. Do you have any clue how many Lady Henriettas have sought to talk my ear off in the past few years?" he joked.

"I'm serious! It was no small task," Lady Havenshire responded incredulously.

"Yes, in fairness, I do have an inkling of who you are, Lady Havenshire. Have you forgotten that lovely introduction Lady Henrietta gave you?" he asked. Her laughter died away to grudging admission.

"I do indeed recall," she nodded. "I had good reason to be scared after that, frankly. Noblemen hear of a single woman with an ailing father, and..."

"Ailing father?" Lord Beckham's dry sense of humor faded to a voice full of deep concern. False tears could be conjured by many a skilled liar, and the aristocracy housed many such liars, but something... something, about the deep sound of his voice, about that face, something about... him, convinced Nadia of his sincerity. "I'm... I'm sorry, for..."

"You've nothing to apologize... for," Nadia's voice grew vulnerable as she thought on her father.

"I know the... pain, I watched my father..." Lord Beckham

shamefully admits. "My sister and I could do nothing to help him."

"Your sister?" Lady Havenshire chimed in curiously. The subject clearly made Lord Beckham uncomfortable, as he shifted about in his chair.

"My elder sister, yes, Catherine. A wonderful... woman," he hesitated. Cold realization churned in Lady Havenshire's stomach.

"Elder sister. Catherine," she repeated skeptically. He, like every man, had benefited from the system she despised... no different from the others. "And I'm guessing that as your father passed, he felt safe, having a male heir, yes?" Lord Beckham's expression grew cross.

"I did not... enjoy, seeing my father die, nor did I enjoy the trouble caused by my sister's--"

"Trouble? Is that what your sister was - a trouble? Women - we're such troubles, aren't we?" Nadia interrupted, her mind afire now.

"No, the trouble was in the manner of inheritance. I had no interest in... in feuding with my sister. I..." Lord Beckham's voice fell away. The conversation ended nearly as abruptly as it had begun; Lady Havenshire, her arms crossed atop her chest, looked away.

It hurt her. It hurt her deeply; she thought she'd found a man different from the others, but that moment had come as a blistering reminder that no man cared for women as equals; none saw them as worthy, and every man benefited from a system that put men on top, even those who wanted not to benefit. She found Lord Beckham handsome, strange; that aura, and that charm, had even opened her up and made her vulnerable.

"I hope we're having a lovely time, are we not?" A chipper voice broke the silence; Lord Perrywise, the addled old man, smiling as he stuck his head between the two of them. "Lord Beckham, so pleased you could make it! We've not seen you in the hallowed halls of the manor here in so long! And paired with such a lovely woman, Lady Havenshire! Your father, he was so excited you'd be here, and..."

How perfectly timely an interference. Lord Perrywise, her father - real life, came crashing back down, and she and Lord Beckham simply sat in tense silence, enduring it.

CHAPTER SIX

Failure.

A rapping at the door pulled Lord Beckham from a stormy reverie; that recurring dream, haunting him again, like a specter floating amid the oak and the glass of Berrewithe Manor, hiding in the high shadows of imposing, vaulted ceilings. His eyes opened, though the hazy stupor of liquor and self-loathing cast a murky shadow over his vision; he clung to the faint memories of his dream, reminding him again, and again, that failure had always been his only reasonable option. He had failed Anna; he had failed the woman who had entranced him, just last night; Lady Havenshire, a woman who felt like none he had ever met. A woman who understood his blasé humor; a woman who had appreciated his heart. A woman he had felt a spark with, like the flash of gold-yellow when flint struck tinder... but the fire, as always, had failed to start. Now, he was certain he would never again see the woman who had lit a candle in his own heart; who had, for a few moments of conversation, connected with him as few ever had.

The rapping continued, and a familiar voice broke through. The night had been cruel to Lord Beckham, and after retreating from the dinner party and its blinding lights, pastel corridors and chortling, foppish gentlemen, he had spent the night thinking on her; thinking on Lady Havenshire, thinking on Anna. And when thoughts came of his own failures, of his inadequacies, the drink began; and rarely did it stop, before the morbid dreams of crushed flowers and a wedding reception stolen by rain reminded him of how he didn't deserve a woman; not

Anna, and certainly not one like the young Lady Havenshire.

"M'lord! It's quite time for afternoon tea, and you've nearly slept all the day!" Ms. Cauthfield excoriated her master through the door. Lord Beckham had little interest in facing today; nor did he very well fancy the idea of facing tomorrow, either. He pretended to ignore the old woman crowing through the door, instead shifting along the sheets. The curtains drawn, the glow of midday crept through cracks in the darkness, alerting him that the day had indeed worn on long without him. It only made him feel far worse; far more useless, having spent all evening thinking on his failures, and now all day sleeping upon them, he had little inclination to spend yet another afternoon lost in those thoughts.

He knew he wouldn't be that lucky, though. She had made an impression... and now she's all he could think upon.

"M'lord! Are you quite alright?" Ms. Cauthfield asked, her knuckles striking the door with such rapidity he wondered if they'd leave scuff marks across its polished surface. He lamented with a groan; as consciousness quickly flooded into his faculties he became quite suddenly and sharply aware of a dolorous throbbing in his temples; he ached tremendously through his legs and arms and even into his core, his entire body run ragged by the demon of self-flagellation via drink. And consciousness only brought to bear the worst of his self-loathing, for now he saw her face; he saw her reaction to him, recounting the strained relationship between he and his sister.

Lady Havenshire reminded him of his sister, in some ways; a worldly woman with thoughts of lands far from England; thoughts of a life different from the one people like she and he had been consigned to. He felt selfish in assessing he, too, had been a prisoner of a life he never wanted - a life thrust upon him by the death of his father. He hated the guilt he felt for how his sister had suffered; he hated being complicit in a system that had hurt her, and had sent her away; that had fractured what had once been a happy family living among the rolling greens and beneath the stormy doldrums of northern England.

Now, he had hurt more than just his sister. He had hurt Lady Havenshire - something that had always, and seems would always, happen. Anna had always been right when she'd left him alone, the priest shaking his head; the gathered guests huddled beneath the arcade, their eyes wide and their faces long. Lord Beckham rolled to his side, pulling the sheets across his head, drowning out the light; drowning out the noise. He thought on her. He couldn't stop.

Lady Havenshire. She deserved far more than he could ever give. Lady Havenshire. A woman who had seen the world. What had he done, cloistered away in his manor towering over the peasantry, to deserve her? What could he offer that a woman who had seen the world would ever desire? Why would a man who benefited from a system built against her deserve her hand? Lady Havenshire. Beautiful, but so out of reach. Lady Havenshire.

"M'lord! Lady Havenshire..." the rest of Ms. Cauthfield's words didn't matter; his mind ringing, he leapt from the bed. At first, he thought he had misunderstood; perhaps his wanting mind had pieced together wanton, disconnected sounds and had simply imagined Ms. Cauthfield saying the name. Nevertheless, he wanted to know; he had to know, if she had indeed said that name. Sprung from the bed, he pulled a robe across his broad, strong chest, holding it tight as he lopsidedly bounded towards the door, his legs uneven, aching with each step as the ghost of last evening's indulgences haunted his being.

"M'lord," Ms. Cauthfield asked in concern, having heard the sudden and jarring sounds of Lord Beckham wobbling through his room to the door. Pulling the portal wide, the sunlight struck him and nearly knocked him back into his lightless abyss, as a demon fleeing the scorching flames of heaven. Recoiling, he shook away the pain and the headache and he focused his glazed gaze on Ms. Cauthfield, who regarded him curiously. "I'm glad to see you awake, m'lord. James informed me you had given to drink last evening."

"What was the name you just said, Ms. Cauthfield?" the duke demanded, eyes narrowed through the sunlight pouring through the manor's tall windows. Ms. Cauthfield regarded him with confusion, and his heart hurt, fearing he had simply imagined this.

"A name, m'lord?"

"You said a name, did you not?" he demanded desperately.

"I apologize, m'lord, I was quite concerned for you. James and a few of the other serving girls had said the same," Ms. Cauthfield insisted, worry in her eyes. "Did you have the dream again?"

"So you didn't say her name, then?" Lord Beckham asked with a certain flirt of madness in his tone. Realization startled Ms. Cauthfield and her expression shifted to surprise.

"Oh, yes! Did you mean my mention of Lady Havenshire?"

"So you did mention her?" Lord Beckham asked, relieved that his mind had not fallen so precipitously to insanity. "What do you have to say of her?"

"Oh, m'lord, I apologize, I didn't mean to bother you with trifles like those," Ms. Cauthfield said dismissively. "I had simply mentioned her in hopes of lifting your spirits, and catching your attention."

"How do you know of her?" Lord Beckham asked, strolling to the window near the staircase. He approached slowly, letting the light filter into his muddied mind bit by bit, so as not to overwhelm his constitution, rendered fragile by a night of drink, all at once. Ms. Cauthfield sighed dismissively.

"Again, I apologize for mentioning these sorts of frivolities, I know how you feel about them," Ms. Cauthfield said by way of disclaimer. "A letter arrived from the Havenshire Manor this morning. Apparently, word passed to the duke there, a lovely but ailing old man, that you had spoken a fair few words of conversation to his daughter." Lord Beckham sighed in response.

"Word passed to him, did it?" he scoffed. Both he and Ms. Cauthfield knew just who had 'passed word'.

"You know just how much Lady Henrietta enjoys hearing herself speak, m'lord, particularly when it comes to matters of gossip at dinner parties. I hadn't known she would be at that particular event last night, m'lord, elseways I would have known some manner of gossip as this would get out, and would have advised against your attendance," Ms. Cauthfield lamented. "I'm certain it's simply Lady Henrietta making mere introductions and pleasantries out to be some grand manner of conspiracy or affair, as she is often willing to do. I apologize for even broaching the subject, m'lord. I simply worried for your health this morning."

"No, you needn't apologize," Lord Beckham responded, considering deeply the possibilities before him. No doubt Lady Henrietta had exaggerated what had happened between he and Lady Havenshire. It struck him with poignancy the predicament Lord Havenshire suffered - he realized the ailing man's desire to marry his daughter off, so as to keep the inheritance of wealth and estate within his family. He gazed across the grasses, watching the farmers work their lands; watching life bustle along the roadways in the small town, off in the distance, on the edges of Berrewithe estate. "What manner of meeting does the Lord Havenshire request?" Ms. Cauthfield seemed taken aback by the question, not having expected her master would be at all interested in the letters and gossip of women like Lady Henrietta.

"I'm... not quite certain, to be honest, m'lord, I didn't think would ask on its contents," Ms. Cauthfield replied. "James, I believe, mentioned words about an inheritance, or a discussion thereof--"

"Of course," the duke responded bitterly, his heart stung.

"I've... well, I've heard rumor that Lord Havenshire's health has... failed, quite rapidly, in the passing months, m'lord," Lady Cauthfield added, standing loyally attentive near the stairwell. Her own thoughts began to suddenly turn on the matter of the inheritance, and the duke's daughter - and she began herself to see an opportunity for her master. "Perhaps, you... could hear him out? I know it's a trivial matter, likely inflated by the impetuous chatter of Lady Henrietta, but... well, I think it might be good for you to speak to him, and to speak again to his daughter. She may be quite a lovely woman."

"She is," Lord Beckham sighed, much to Ms. Cauthfield's wide-eyed surprise. "She's worldly, capable, intelligent, stunning. She's what one would want and expect of a true noblewoman," Lord Beckham lamented. Surprised to hear words such as those coming from her master, Ms. Cauthfield's voice grew urgent.

"So, it's not simple hearsay or gossip from Lady Henrietta? M'lord, certainly you'll go and see the duke and his daughter, then?" she asked, hopefully.

"No, I shan't," Lord Beckham said in disappointment, deflating his servant.

"And why is that? You've just spoken highly of the woman, and her father clearly needs your assistance," Ms. Cauthfield insisted.

"I've offended her, and I certainly don't deserve a second chance by speaking with her dying father behind her back. She shall certainly regard me then as up to no good, looking to steal from her agency and her fortune without regard for who she is," Lord Beckham reasoned. "No. I've failed already in regard to lovely Lady Havenshire."

"Oh, come now," Ms. Cauthfield chastised. "You've earned the interest of her father, and no matter what sort of offense she's taken from you, she'd be foolish not to recognize your merits as a gentleman."

"But I'm not a gentleman, am I?" Lord Beckham protested. "A gentleman doesn't fail his love as I have. A gentleman doesn't estrange his sister, offend women like Lady Havenshire."

"M'lord, I've held back from speaking so cross as I wish about Lady Anna in the past, but if I must I shall be blunt as a blacksmith's hammer," Ms. Cauthfield said, full of fire. "You did not fail Lady Anna. She failed you. You treated her as angels deserve, yet she left you suffering on what should have been the finest day in Berrewithe Manor's history. And why? Why, m'lord?"

"I wasn't enough," Lord Beckham insisted, brooding as he watched the sun through the windows.

"She used you, m'lord. She used you for her own selfish ends, and when she had no more a need of you, she abandoned you. You had far more to offer than she was ever worth," Ms. Cauthfield roared. Lord Beckham hesitated. He wouldn't hear it; he wouldn't face that thought.

"Ms. Cauthfield, I'd ask you to mind your place," he said defensively.

"At least listen to the old man. He's dying, m'lord," Ms. Cauthfield pleaded, at the edge of her patience.

"Prepare a carriage," he muttered. "I suppose I shall at least hear him out... if only for the reputation of the manor. Of Berrewithe," he tried to rationalize.

Truly, all he wanted was to her see her face again.

CHAPTER SEVEN

"I don't believe I've ever taken you this far from the manor, have I?" James, the old butler, asked, driving the horses along the roadway. Lord Beckham had requested a simple carriage, and for James to accompany him, expecting the trip would be short; he would speak to the ailing lord, perhaps ask on the matter of inheritance, politely refuse the ailing lord's offer, and board the carriage back to his manor. Instead the trip had been long, dull; James had spent much of it trying, full of hope, to pry from his master the events of the past evening. Lord Beckham knew all of his servants hoped to have a new woman at the manor - and he deftly avoided the subject at every encounter, not wanting to let down his loyal butler by informing him that Lady Havenshire had left rather upset.

"I'm not certain," Lord Beckham said lackadaisically, looking on the moors and thinking.

"I recall taking your sister all the way to London," James laughed, before an uncomfortable feeling settled across the both of them. The duke watched the roadway, troubled, taking deep breaths as he considered his own past. "I do... sometimes quite miss your sister, m'lord. Begging your pardon, of course, her manner of leaving us was..."

"It was perfect justified, James," Lord Beckham rumbled, the self-loathing flaring once more as he recalled the last few days he spent with his sister.

"We... we simply had to follow the law of the land. For the better of the estate, and the memory of your father. None of us wanted to,"

James recalled, "but... there was little we could do, after the magistrate demanded you inherit, over Leah."

"Does that not trouble you, James?" Lord Beckham asked, confrontational.

"You're quite a capable, intelligent man, and a good master to have, m'lord. Your sister had all those, of course, but she... well, she was a woman," James lamented.

"Does that trouble you? The thought of having a woman as a master? As the woman in charge of Berrewithe? Of the estate?" Lord Beckham challenged.

"Oh, certainly not," James murmured, the horse hooves slowing as the carriage wound through the forested lands at the edge of the Havenshire estate. "I've no trouble listening to Ms. Cauthfield with each waning day!" he laughed. "Though... it's, well... it's simply not how our world works, m'lord."

"Don't you think we ought to pontificate on changing that, James? Isn't a woman worth as much as I am? Perhaps more?"

"I... I hadn't... thought on it, m'lord," James answered slowly.

"Perhaps you should. Perhaps all of England should."

"That's quite curious talk," James said, a little surprised. "I've... I suppose I am an old man. Our ways are our ways. I would not... mind a change, but I haven't quite thought about one."

"If we had thought on one, as a society, perhaps we could change things. Perhaps Leah would not have left in disgust, on seeing this world for what it could truly be. Is it gentlemanly, James, to disregard the value women have in our society?" Lord Beckham challenged.

"I'm not... certain, m'lord. I... I suppose I leave those sorts of thoughts up to men far wiser than I," James chuckled uncomfortably. The duke decided not to press his servant any further, sitting in silence, and instead contemplating the questions on his own. Had he deserved the family fortune over his beloved sister simply because he had been born a man? Was Lady Havenshire right to be offended by a system that allowed such a thing to happen? Did he truly deserve the position he held - or had it simply been gifted to him by the circumstances of his birth?

"We're nearly here, m'lord," James announced, pulling round the front of the manor. Though not quite as impressive as Berrewithe, its wrought-iron gates and gardens impressed Marshall, who found servants waiting at the door to greet him. "I suppose I shall wait?" James asked.

"It shouldn't be long, James," Lord Beckham said, nodding as he exited the simple, wooden carriage. Approaching the door with a stern expression, Lord Beckham met with the welcoming eyes of a portly old man and a stern elderly woman, who quite reminded him of a harsher sort of Ms. Cauthfield.

"Welcome, Lord Beckham, to Emerys, and to Lord Havenshire's manor," the older woman said, nodding. "I'm Ms. Mulwray, and this is Egan. We'd be delighted to take you to the--"

"Excuse me, yes, it's a pleasure, but I'm in quite a bit of a haste," Lord Beckham insisted. A sudden urgency filled his head; he realized all at once just where he had arrived, and who lived inside. He recalled her face - beautiful, but vexed the last he had seen it. Vexed with pained thoughts and regret. He knew, in his heart, he shouldn't have come; any time he blinked, he saw only flashes of his painful day, his dashed wedding in the Delshire Moors.

"Apologies, then, Lord Beckham," the old woman said, a slight irritation in her tone. "Let me lead you to the dining room, then, where you'll find Lord Havenshire waiting to discuss a matter of some importance." The portly man bowed courteously to Lord Beckham as he passed through the doors, the wooded interior rather inviting and every surface polished to a gleam. Maidservants cluttered the furnished foyer, their eyes alight with impish curiosity as they saw the dark man pass through the entryway. The doors swung open to a cavernous dining hall, with lanterns lit low and curtains drawn across the fading daylight beaming through short, squat windows. At the end of the table, he saw what looked like a withered husk of a man - skin pale, his body clearly ravaged with pain as he struggled to appear welcoming, with lifting his arms quite an exhausting task for the man, his hair spotty and gray.

"Lord Beckham! I've not had the pleasure of welcoming you to the manor yet," Lord Havenshire announced, before a spat of coughs interrupted his words. Lady Henrietta sat at the pained man's flank, sipping on a cup of tea, her eyelids fluttering innocently at Lord Beckham, though he could see the conspiratorial glint in her gaze. Humbly Lord Beckham bowed, crossing wordlessly through the threshold and towards the two of them.

"A pleasure indeed," Lord Beckham finally said, and only then upon coming close to Lord Havenshire did he realize just how dire the situation was for the lord. Lady Henrietta remained silent - a rarity for her - though the little smile on her face said all that she wanted to say, letting Lord Beckham know she had been the little bird whispering in Lord Havenshire's ear about the meeting between Nadia and Marshall the night before.

"A friend of mine, Lady Henrietta," Lord Beckham introduced.

"Oh, we're quite the friends, aren't we, Marshall?" Lady Henrietta beamed, clearly quite proud of having tried her hand at playing matchmaker between lords and ladies. She clearly appeared to think Lord Beckham would appreciate the gesture, just as clearly as she clearly expected he would thank her profusely for finding him a potential wife. Instead, his words remained hasty.

"Yes, I know Lady Henrietta well, and I'm quite certain I know why I've been asked to come to the estate, m'lord," Lord Beckham nodded to the older man, who smiled wide, always wearing the mask of confidence in spite of his condition. "However, I'm not certain I'm the man you're looking for, for Nadia." That statement shocked Lady Henrietta, whose expression turned at once from smug satisfaction to mild frustration.

"Oh, come now darling, you're certainly underselling yourself! Now's the time to oversell yourself," Lady Henrietta chortled. "Lord Havenshire's invited you to speak on a great many things, hasn't he?" she looked hopeful towards the lord, who himself seemed at a loss for words. He certainly wasn't used to men so blatant in their desire - or lack thereof - to court his daughter.

"Lady Henrietta," he said, his flight instincts urging him to flee, as the bitter memories of Anna flooded his every sense, "I sincerely appreciate you introducing me to Lord Havenshire, but I'm... well, my meeting last evening with Lady Havenshire was most pleasant, but--"

"Of course it was! She's a lovely girl, and you made quite an impression, didn't you? I could see the smile on her face," Lady

Henrietta insisted. "Now, you've been invited here to have a pleasant conversation, and it'd be quite crass to refuse Lord Havenshire that, wouldn't it?"

"Lady Henrietta," Marshall again insisted firmly, "I have to say, you didn't quite see the full extent of Lady Havenshire and I's interaction. I'm not certain you know what happened, and for that reason I have to ask you to... kindly, keep quiet," Lord Beckham said, eliciting a shocked gasp from Lady Henrietta.

"Marshall! I've worked quite diligently to convince Lord Havenshire to invite you here," Lady Henrietta squealed. "Now, it's quite insulting of you to deny his hospitality! Lord Havenshire, I apologize, but I--"

"I've got an idea," Lord Havenshire interjected diplomatically with a faint smile. "No offense, Lady Henrietta, but I've something I really want to show Lord Beckham. Alone. How about we go out to the stables and I show you the family horses? Nadia's quite enamored with them, and I think it'd give us a chance to talk," he finished; Lord Beckham heard Lady Henrietta let out a loud humph.

"I'm... not certain, I've quite a lot to attend to at my estate, and I had hoped to make this meeting rather hasty," Lord Beckham said hesitantly. He looked at Lord Havenshire, and felt a guilt in his throat.

"It won't take long at all," Lord Havenshire insisted brightly, before another coughing fit filled his throat. "Not long at all." Lord Beckham sighed.

"Yes, perhaps we should," he finally relented.

CHAPTER EIGHT

"She's a beauty, isn't she?" Lord Havenshire asked, his voice a hoarse whisper as he loudly cleared his throat. Lord Beckham couldn't stand the smell of stables; he wasn't himself much enamored with horses, for that matter, something that had he spoke it aloud would have met with much surprise and alarm. Few men here among the moors of north England didn't appreciate horses or the art of riding them, but the pursuit had never quite earned Lord Beckham's interest. The heady stench of hay and the low whinny of chattering equines inspired only a sidelong gaze from Marshall, who regarded the animal Lord Havenshire presented proudly with a faint but clearly disinterested smile.

"Yes, indeed, a fine breed," Lord Beckham returned absentmindedly. Its skin a deep shade of brown and its hair long and white, Lord Beckham got the feeling that these were perhaps special or rare features for a horse to have, or that they were quite prominent and agreeable on this particular horse, but he knew so little of horses that he couldn't point out the differences between a beautiful and a rather mundane example of the animal. He glanced longing towards the stable doors, sighing deeply and begging silently for James to pull the carriage away from the roadway and off to the stables to rescue him.

"When's the last time you went riding, Lord Beckham?" Lord Havenshire asked with a knowing grin, offering the animal to Marshall, who recoiled at the offer. He hadn't ridden a horse in so long he couldn't even recall the last occasion, save that it likely ended with him nearly thrown from the animal's back, as he found himself to rarely have what it took to control the wily creatures. He quite rightly feared embarrassing himself should the old man actually ask to have a ride.

"Not many opportunities for a ride at my estate, I'm afraid," Lord Beckham answered, reeling from the smell and the sight of the stabled animal that approached him willfully. "It's... rather rocky terrain, near the manor," Lord Beckham resolved an excuse as quickly as he could for his lacking equestrian skills. Lord Havenshire frowned.

"Unfortunate, that. I've always found the freedom of riding the back of one of these beauties to be one of the most liberating experiences our mortal existence has to offer us, and these last few months without a ride across my property have left me begging to feel that again," Lord Havenshire lamented. "Alas, the illness has made me too weak to control one of the animals, I'm rather ashamed to admit. The Emerys estate has quite the perfect sort of landscape for a good ride. Horses aren't quite enamored with the trees, of course, but they weave through them far easier than they would rocks or soaring mountains, or that sort of thing."

"Indeed," Lord Beckham responded idly, still vexed as he glanced towards the stable doors. A dozen horses stood arrayed along the wooden walls, each sequestered into its own quaint den, stuffed with buckets of water, bales of straw and plates of assorted vegetables and other manner of detritus for the creatures to feast upon. Lord Beckham recalled his own manor's stables, sitting empty and idle upon his land since he'd sold the last of the creatures to a home which had actual want and use of them; he himself had no such needs.

"My daughter, Nadia... this is her horse, Shadow. They grew up together, practically," Lord Havenshire laughed, his voice both joyous, proud, but momentarily heartbroken at recalling his daughter's youth. "They taught one another how to ride, and how to run, more or less. She's always been an exceptional rider, so much so that had she not been born the only daughter of a duke, I'd have told her to pursue her riding skill relentlessly," he joked. "She may well do so, regardless. She's always been stubborn about listening to the ramblings of her old father."

"She... certainly seemed willful," Lord Beckham recalled hesitantly. "But... a charming sort of willful."

"A charming sort indeed," Lord Havenshire laughed. "It's my own fault, letting her range freely across the world like a wandering little chicken pecking at seeds on a plain. I fear it's made her unmarriageable, seeing the world outside of this place. I wake up each day fearing my servants will inform me she's disappeared on Shadow's back, into the night," he sighed.

"I certainly don't think a woman doesn't deserve marriage because she can think for herself," Lord Beckham responded, earning a curious look from Lord Havenshire.

"Had she been born a man, she'd be the finest duke Emerys has ever seen," he lamented.

"And do you think that's a problem of her birth? Or a problem of how we do things here?" Lord Beckham presented the question with a tap on his chin.

"Now you're beginning to sound like her," Lord Havenshire guffawed, before a coughing fit stole his breath away. He slunk onto one of the stable keeper's stools. "She's quite the firebrand, and I know the other gentlemen... they see no value in a woman who's been across the world. They think she's... mad, or that some ill-mannered ideas have tainted her like a disease," Lord Havenshire lamented.

"She certainly seemed... lovely, when I spoke with her," Lord Beckham hesitated to say, though he meant it.

"That," Lord Havenshire exclaimed, "that. Is precisely why I've invited you here, Marshall. You know how our world works - even if it's not how we want it to work, not how Nadia wants it to work. If you could just, perhaps, help to teach her - help to convince her, that while the idea of women as equals is noble... it's just not how it works. Coming from you--"

"Father? The servants told me you'd gone to the stables," a voice crept through the stable doors; Lord Beckham's heart froze, his eyes widened. He heard her - her pleasant but plucky voice, and with his eyes set on the swinging stable doors, he saw her, dressed in the manner of an equestrian, her pants tight and tall and white, clung to her sweet curves, her expression bright, her hair tied back, a jacket fit snug over her torso. Her eyes gleamed... until they fell upon the sight of Lord Beckham, a familiar face that inspired so many different, clashing emotions in her mind. She swallowed hard, her own expression mirroring the shock in Lord Beckham's.

He appreciated seeing her... even if it came at so disastrous a time.

"Nadia! You recognize this man, don't you? Lady Henrietta told me you two had quite a time sitting next to one another last night at Lord Perrywise's banquet," Lord Havenshire exclaimed in the loudest, congratulatory tone his ravaged throat could muster. "I've invited him to see the horses, and I was just exhibiting Shadow to him."

"Y... yes, I know of... of Lord Beckham," Nadia gulped, watching Marshall closely. He regarded her with his own sense of suspicion, of praise; he had no inkling of how offended she had been after their failed conversation, or even if he had any hope to make good their potential relationship. "I'm not certain what Lady Henrietta believed of our relationship, but... we're simply acquaintances, nothing more," she said, rather cuttingly.

"Y... yes, acquaintances," Lord Beckham responded, crestfallen.

"And is here to purchase a horse, then?" Nadia asked curtly. "...with the fortune he secured from beneath his sister's feet?"

"Lady Havenshire, I had hoped we could speak about--" Lord Beckham blurted, ire stoked by her comments.

"Speak about? Speak about what?" she retorted, arms crossed atop her chest.

"Nadia, you're not being courteous to our guest," Lord Havenshire rumbled. "Act like a proper lady, I know for certain I and Ms. Mulwray taught you properly."

"Guest? He's a guest, is he?" Lady Havenshire scowled. "I'm not quite so stupid as you seem to believe, father. I've guessed astutely at the purpose of his visit, and I'm quite certain it's not simply to fawn over the horses."

"That's not how I taught you to speak to your peers, Nadia," Lord Havenshire grumbled, coughing as he shifted along the uncomfortable stool.

"M'lady, I had no intentions of offending you, but I was scarcely going to simply ignore the plea of a sick man to visit his estate, whether

Lady Henrietta was behind it or no," Lord Beckham protested. "I apologize for offense my situation may have caused your sensibilities, but--"

"But you knew you had offended me, yet you accepted my father's invitation, knowing full well who had had a hand in it, and what he - and Lady Henrietta - had hoped would come from such a meeting," Nadia bristled, her long equestrian boot stamping into the dirt as she punctuated each word harshly. "Taking that into account, I don't think you're quite sorry for your words or situation at all. I think you're taking full advantage of the position afforded you as a man."

"I had no intention of offending you, again," Lord Beckham growled, "but I'd be betraying myself and my estate if I so crassly refused--"

"Such simple excuses," Nadia scoffed.

"Nadia, I've invited this man to our estate and now you're insulting him, and I'll not tolerate it," Lord Havenshire's voice gurgled out through a cough.

"Father, you've invited this man to try to marry me off, just as you called me back home to marry me off. And now, you're conspiring to take away my agency, simply because you think it'd be in my best interests. And how are you to say I'm not capable of acting in my own best interests? I'm a grown woman, with a mind, one that's seen far more of the world than a man like this," she sneered, before turning in disgust and storming from the stable door. Deflated, Lord Beckham realized he had, by now, done too much damage to any hope he had held on to reignite that spark; to strike the flint once more and create a raging fire of emotion between them. He had failed, just as he had failed Anna.

"You see what a dying old father has to deal with?" Lord Havenshire coughed loudly, shaking his head. "She's lovely, really, beneath the layers of willful scorn she wears like heavy plate armor, I promise. She takes from me - not her mother, who was as lovely a woman as the moors have ever seen. No, I was willful as she is when I was her age, and I blame myself for letting the world change her, make her hardened, and not the woman she should be, looking for a husband," he lamented. "I apologize for her."

"You needn't," Lord Beckham shook his head. "Willful, yes, and perhaps far too judgmental for her own good. But I would never fault a woman for thinking of her own freedom. Isn't that what all men do?" Lord Havenshire regarded him curiously, still stunned to hear these sorts of things said by a man of northern England.

"Lord Beckham, I have to be brutal in my honesty to you. I've not told anyone, not even Nadia, but... I've not got much time of my own left on this world. She's not stupid, and so I'm certain she grasps the urgency of my situation, but she... Ms. Mulwray, they've all deluded themselves into denial. The truth is that without some manner of intervention, I'll die without seeing her married, and she - and our family estate - will be lost," Lord Havenshire confided, his voice shaky. "You, though - you've shown an unusual sort of tolerance for my daughter's ideas, and... well, I can't be certain what was said between you, at that dinner, but I think that you're the only man I can say this to, right now, in confidence that you'll understand."

"It's gracious of you to trust me, m'lord, but..." Lord Beckham hesitated; he heard thunder begin to rumble, and as the sound stretched across the sea of grass waving beyond, he swallowed, flashes of the day on the Delshire Moors bringing fresh trauma to his mind. "...I'm not deserving of your daughter; or of any wife, in honesty. I've only disappointed those I've fallen in love with, and I've no doubt your daughter - finding herself a prisoner in her estate - would fare any better."

"A disappointment? Marshall, you're anything but," Lord Havenshire insisted. "Your tolerance for my daughter's odd ideas means you're the only man I've known capable of corralling her. Of convincing her of the importance of marriage."

"I..." Lord Beckham's voice trailed away as he thought on the old man's words. Perhaps Lord Havenshire had a point. Lord Beckham knew the sorts of men cluttering the aristocracy; outwardly they loved to play the role of the deferential gentleman, but within they harbored all those same predilections and basal passions that drove all the misery and woe of the world - greed for power, greed for control; greed for wealth and fortune. He knew she needed marriage - even if she didn't want it - and she knew that any other man would keep her in the cage she feared, and would stifle all those thoughts of hers.

"Lord Beckham, I beg you to at least, please consider the thought. I know how Nadia appears, but she's a lovely woman," Lord Havenshire pleaded, tears rolling at the edges of his eyes. With a weighty sigh, Lord Beckham glanced away, holding his eyes closed.

"I'll... consider it, m'lord," he answered in a deep, thrumming tone. "I'll... I'll consider it closely."

CHAPTER NINE

What nerve he'd had!

Lady Havenshire had lost the inclination to go riding; while it had always been one of her favorite pastimes, and she looked forward to her first afternoon spent atop her trusted steed Shadow, the sight of her father and that lord conspiring to usurp her individuality had put her off the stables; off of quite a bit of everything. Instead she stood now at the top of the stairwell, glancing down into the foyer, with her helmet, jacket and jodhpurs replaced by a flowing white gown and her messy hair falling across her shoulder, she waited indignantly for her father to return from the stables. She had quite a lot she wanted to say to him, even if it vexed her to think of his poor condition and how he had truly wanted the best for her.

But how could he or anyone other than her, know what she most wanted in the world?

The nerve, that Lord Beckham must've had, to answer a summons after last night. They'd spoken, and she'd realized he had been the same as every other man - always happy to step atop a woman to elevate themselves, even their own mothers, daughters, and sisters. Their conversation had been nil after that particular exchange; she had no real interest in entertaining more words from a man who had benefited so crassly from the institutions she hated. Lady Henrietta had poked her head in between the two of them from time to time...

Lady Henrietta! Lady Havenshire's rage only grew as she thought on how this had all come to pass. No doubt that insufferable old woman had gotten into her father's ear just last night, crowing on about how wonderful the event had been; how Nadia had been chattering on with a lord whom Lady Henrietta thought to be a suitable suitor. This had all been her doing, hadn't it? Fuming, Nadia stared intently at the door, arming herself with one argument, and then another, preparing to eviscerate her father's own arguments about her fate and about Lord Beckham.

She had not been completely without base in making such assumptions. Of course, he had benefited from a crooked system, he had stepped over his sister! But Lady Havenshire had not failed to give him credit for his charms; for his open mind. He had made her laugh, after all; something none in England had managed in earnest for quite some time. His voice commanding, she could even appreciate how handsome he was; something she had long ago given up on finding properly in England. He had certainly been different from the others... but not so different, she reassured herself. As attractive, and interesting, as the man had proven, she wouldn't become just another woman like her friends, giving up their minds and wills to marry for inheritance and social gain.

Curious maidservants scrambled about the polished furniture and the long shadows of nightfall crossing through the foyer, their eyes flashing over angry Lady Havenshire, words of lilted gossip passing across their tongues. Nadia crossed her arms, her expression cross, as she watched the doors to the manor open slowly, a thunderstorm brewing without, rumbles echoing across the trees and grasses of the Emerys estate.

"I've good news," the tired duke announced as he closed the door behind him. "Lord Beckham has expressed a potential interest in courting you, Nadia."

"Did you see him off, then?" Nadia asked her father, ignoring his proud pronouncement, as he tiredly crossed the threshold. "Is he going back to his estate?" he lifted his gaze, his face weary; she felt a twinge of concern for her father in his heart, knowing that he had spent more time out of bed trying to impress today than he likely had in the months since he'd fallen ill.

"Nadia," he responded, his voice weak, "I had invited Lord Beckham here as a guest. I have respected you, my daughter, for your impudence for quite a long time, but treating my guests in this manner... it's not acceptable."

"He was no ordinary guest, father, and it's insulting of you to lie to me in such a manner," Nadia fumed. "I know just why you invited him, and I know just why agreed to come here. Lady Henrietta has been singing quite melodically into your ear all night and all day, hasn't she, father?"

"Lady Henrietta sings quite a great many tunes into my ear each day, Nadia, do you think I listen to every bit of gossip she blurts out?" her father responded harshly, dragging himself slowly towards the stairs.

"I think she mentioned the possibility of pairing me off with some man, and you leapt at the opportunity, having your courier send a message all the way to Berrewithe before dawn had even broken," Nadia sniped back.

"I work with haste because I haven't got all the time in the world to assure your future, and the future of my family and estate, is secure,"

Lord Havenshire rumbled in response. He began to scale the stairwell, one step at a time, each step a monumental task of its own.

"Father, please, you speak with so much certainty when you say that," Nadia retorted sharply.

"I speak with certainty because it is a certainty," her father exclaimed. "It is a certainty I will die - whether sooner, or later, and it is a certainty that when I do, my estate - my life, everything - either falls into your hands, or you lose everything; all of the servants lose everything. Do you know how precarious I feel, in this position?" he shuddered as he bounded another step, rain beginning to pour against the windowpanes.

"Father, have you ever considered my own thoughts and feelings in your calculations about this estate? About the inheritance? When you called me back to England, did that matter to you? What I wanted? Is it so selfish of your daughter to want the freedom that you've always enjoyed, father?" Nadia said, her voice warbling as the seriousness of her father's condition began to set in.

"Nadia, I have always thought about your feelings," Lord Havenshire croaked, "from the moment I watched you born; watched you grow. I would change our world if I could, but that's too much effort for one dying, old man," he continued, breathlessly; he nearly collapsed half-way up the stairs, falling to one knee with a groan. Nadia gasped, rushing spiritedly down the stairs to her father's side, slinging his arm over her shoulder and lifting him.

"Father, please, be careful, don't hurt yourself," she whispered, hefting him up as best she could. "You need to rest. We'll... we'll get past this," she murmured, her own hope about her father's condition beginning to fade away as tears stained red rivulets along her cheeks.

"Nadia, I've only ever wanted to help you, my daughter," Lord Havenshire said, tone full of regret.

"I know father, I know," she assured him tearfully.

"Lord... Lord Beckham, he seems a good man, and more than anything, he's... he's the sort of man who will indulge you, indulge your thoughts, and your fantasies, bless him," her father laughed, as they scaled another step together.

"H... how do you mean?" Nadia questioned, confused, hoisting her father up another stair as a flash of lightning streaked across their faces.

"Something Lady Henrietta said caught my ear, and it's the only reason I agreed to see this man, to judge him, Nadia," Lord Havenshire said, his voice having fallen to a wobbly whisper. "She said... she said she saw him make you laugh. Nadia, my love, I've not seen you laugh from the joke or foible of a man since you were so young that you laughed at everything," he confided in her. "If he had made you laugh... something, in your hearts, I knew... I knew he would... he would be right, for..." he had begun to give in to his fatigue, his words growing delirious. "He... he believes you, in your... your words, about, about women, but..."

"Father, please, you're tired, save your strength," Nadia whispered. One step left, and her knees nearly buckled as she lifted her father, whose legs had given in and whose body had become a heavy, limp mass of disease-ravaged flesh. Ms. Mulwray emerged from the hall lead to the master bedroom, her face full of concern.

"M'lord?" she asked frightfully, rushing to aid Nadia by slinging her master's other arm across her shoulders.

"He'll be fine, Ms. Mulwray, he's simply exhausted," Nadia whispered.

"I warned him, I told him Egan and I and Lady Henrietta could speak with this suitor and report to him, he needn't trouble himself," Ms. Mulwray hissed. "I warned him..."

"He wanted to help me, in his own way," Nadia sighed, her tears slowing. They hobbled together with her drowsy father through the corridor to the darkened room, lightning flashing again as rain pattered hard against the roof, pouring down and filling all the crevices and cracks, with droplets coalescing into little running rivers of rainwater. They crept through the darkness, gently laying the aging man out onto the bed, carefully covering his body with a blanket, lighting a small candle to provide some source of light in utter darkness.

"He cares so much for you, for us - for the estate, m'lady," Ms. Mulwray said in her stern manner. "He's done more than you can know. Don't let him suffer with--"

"It's quite alright, Ms. Mulwray," her father spoke up, startling the two women. "My daughter is just... willful, is she not?" he smiled drowsily, barely able to open his eyes. He took Nadia's hand; she squeezed his.

"She's very much that," Ms. Mulwray said, her eyes still scaring as she watched the two of them. "Do you need anything, m'lord?"

"No, Ms. Mulwray, thank you, just leave my daughter and I for a moment," he implored. With venom in her glare she briefly and sternly regarded Nadia before spinning wordlessly and leaving the bedroom.

"Sometimes I fear Ms. Mulwray has it in for me," Nadia joked.

"Oh, come now, you know she hasn't, she's simply protective of me, the old woman," Lord Havenshire laughed. "Very protective of the estate. She doesn't like willful women. Thinks they ought to be in their proper place. Not the sort of thing you'd ever agree with," he laughed a croaking, hoarse and painful laugh.

"Certainly not, no," Nadia smiled.

"I... I only ever wanted to help you, Nadia, and I hope you realize that," the crestfallen lord confided. "I know how you feel, about men, about life here, but... I really think Lord Beckham is different from the others. I think you might... actually come to love him." Her heart clashed with itself; she wanted to listen to her father, but the subject of that man burned with so much confusion inside of her.

"What... did he say? About me, about women?" she couldn't stave off that curiosity any longer, and it nagged at her. He had taken advantage of this system that favored him - what could he possibly know about the struggles of woman simply seeking to be equal?

"He'll be able to tell you himself, what he thinks of women, next week," Lord Havenshire said. "I've accepted, on your behalf, an invitation to his manor for a nice dinner, between just the two of you."

"You what?" Nadia asked incredulously, her hesitation boiling over in to mild anger. "Father, I never agreed to such a thing. He may be what you say he is, even, but I don't..."

"Just give him a chance, won't you? You might be surprised. He's not the arrogant, greedy animal you might think he is," Lord Havenshire implored.

"Father, I... I want my freedom. Any man, in this system, is going to want to control me - don't you understand that? No man, no matter how good his heart, is going to work against the way this society favors him," Nadia insisted.

"You take such a dim view of the world, for so beautiful and capable a woman, Nadia," Lord Havenshire said. "Listen to him... you might be surprised."

She doubted she would.

"For your sake, father," she grudgingly admitted. "For your sake."

CHAPTER TEN

Her father had begged her to listen; to keep her mind open. After another week of thought and struggle, Nadia had already made up her mind.

Women aren't supposed to ride; that's what the stable keeper had told her. Ms. Mulwray had had her own brand of looking down her nose at Nadia, constantly lording over the poor girl and chastising her for disobeying her ailing father, or sometimes for showing any sort of thought or initiative whatsoever. She'd had a whole week to deal with the same sorts of issues she'd dealt with her whole life - the preconceptions and the greed she dealt with as a prisoner of her own womanhood - that by the time Egan had hitched up the horses and readied the carriage to carry her across the moors and through the forests and to Lord Beckham's doorway, she had already decided precisely how she planned to deal with the dinner her father had arranged with the mysterious man.

She had no interest in him - no interest in any man who would continue to benefit from the warped power structure that the aristocracy placed on the burdened shoulders of the workers and the women like her. She'd sit; she'd be perfectly personable. She'd say as little as she needed to, eat as little as she needed to; she'd keep her integrity, and she'd leave. That'd be the end of it, she decided; and her father, as much as she loved him, would have to deal with it.

"You're going to try to have at least a bit of fun, right, m'lady?" Egan implored, interrupting the jaunty tune he had been whistling the entire ride from the gates of Emerys to the rocky roadways leading in to Lord Beckham's estate in Berrewithe. Lady Havenshire remained obstinate, responding in as few words as she could.

"Perhaps, Egan," she lied; she knew precisely what she planned to do, and none of it involved 'fun'. Living a week, a few weeks; any weeks, really, as a woman with a will of her own would never be fun. It had been fun carousing in Canada, and India, and even in the United States; it had been fun, being her own, free person, without the burdens of warped expectations on her shoulders. Now, she knew she'd have no fun again, unless a man decided for he she was allowed to have it.

"That didn't sound very confident," Egan's endless insight provided. "You'll at least give the food a good try, right? I'm curious how the house staff's cooking measures up to Ms. Ranold's usual dinners."

"I preferred your whistling, Egan," Lady Havenshire responded, nonplussed.

"If I recall quite rightly, m'lady, one of the last trips of ours evolved into a rather pointed conversation of how you couldn't stand my whistling very much," Egan quipped. "Am I to take it as a compliment that you're pleased to hear my tunes again, m'lady?" he asked facetiously.

"Take it how you like, Egan," she sniped, and quite obnoxiously, Egan began to whistle again. Like an angry child Lady Havenshire simply bore it, too proud to object. The carriage began to hit rather rough patches of terrain, the horses whinnying and the wagon-wheels creaking; she found herself tilted back against the bench, carried slowly up the side of a rather steep hill, as deep clouds broke to reveal a simmering orange sunset on the horizon. She peeked from inside the vehicle to see the estate of Lord Beckham - its appearance, the sun behind it cresting down through cottony gray-black clouds, taking the girl's breath away.

"Quite a place," Egan said in surprise, stopping even the whistle of his sarcastic tune, simply beholding the manor. "I'm not certain where you may have met this man, m'lady, but her certainly seems prepared to entertain."

"Yes," Lady Havenshire said, turning away and ignoring her own surprise at the manor. He was still just a man, and she wouldn't ignore or forget or be charmed out of making the point she had come here to make today. She crossed her arms, looking instead at the sweeping, rocky hills dotting the estate, a landscape nearly as stormy as the man she remembered from that night - his expression entrancing, but mysterious; concealing beneath someone charming and funny, but clearly troubled. She couldn't dispel all those curious thoughts she had of him, no matter how hard she tried, so she instead ignored them as best she could and tried to maintain her focus on her mission.

"You know, he may not be the greedy scoundrel you think he is, m'lady," Egan whispered conspiratorially.

"That's quite enough, Egan," Lady Havenshire said in a huff, ignoring the beautiful, palatial estate before her. Egan chuckled, driving the horses around the bend and leading the carriage to the doors of the estate.

"Announcing the Lady Havenshire," Egan boomed, pulling the door to the carriage open for her. She hesitantly lifted her ornate, white-blue gown and carefully stepped out of the vehicle, exhaling softly and looking around. Once more the stormy gleam of the manor caught her eye; as darkly enticing as the man she had met that night. She quickly tried to compose herself, wearing her most uninviting expression, as she marched stridently towards the front door of the manor.

"Have fun, m'lady," Egan imparted on her as she left, much to her chagrin. She prepared to open the vast entryway doors, until they flew open before her, bright and inviting faces there to receive the lady.

"Hello and welcome! It's been such a long time since we've played host to such a lovely personage," came the warm and comforting voice of an old woman ushering Nadia out of the cool sunset and into the darkly-paneled, richly-appointed halls of the estate. "I'm Ms. Cauthfield, head of staff here at Berrewithe Manor, and it's an utter joy to host your arrival, m'lady," The old woman insisted, taking the lady's hand and leading her past plush couches, maple tables and gold-trimmed accoutrements. "Lord Beckham has anticipated your arrival all week! We've been preparing endlessly to ensure everything's just as you like it."

Nadia quietly admitted that this... was certainly not what she expected, not when coming to the manor of a stormy man, on a rocky moor, possessed by ghosts of his own past. She had expected... well, frankly, she had expected a woman to shout at her in much the manner she had grown used to dealing with, as she had with Ms. Mulwray. Instead, Ms. Cauthfield appeared to be something of a kindred heart. Her own defenses still starkly drawn up, she couldn't help but be impressed by the beautiful art paneling the halls of the manor as Ms. Cauthfield led her through.

"Is that a piece by Madame Gerard?" Nadia blinked, utterly

stunned to see Parisian art adorning the house of a man as dour as the one she remembered.

"You know your art, do you?" Ms. Cauthfield smiled. "Lord Beckham has an eye for the finest painters you'll find in much of Europe, and elsewhere."

"I spent time in Paris," Lady Havenshire recalled, momentarily awestruck. She tried to reel back her surprise, briefly forgetting she had come here to rebuff the man and all he stood for. Instead, she found herself admiring his art as they strolled towards his dining room.

The doors to the dining hall flew open, cool lights dimly illuminating a table covered in ornate candelabras and a gold-trimmed tablecloth. It took her a long moment to take in the wondrous look - and the wealth it must have taken to assemble something so luxurious.

"Lord Beckham's quite excited to see you," Ms. Cauthfield insisted, pulling out a chair for her to sit in - it was taller than she, its wood-carvings hand-painted, weaving beautiful flowery patterns among overstuffed, plush cushions. "He's quite pleased to have you. Is everything to your liking, m'lady?" the old woman asked gleefully.

"I'm... yes, quite, Ms. Cauthfield," Nadia said, a quiet and incredulous laugh in her voice. "I... well, I simply didn't expect this. Given, you see, what I've known of your master, thus far."

"I know how he can come across as," Ms. Cauthfield explained, "but we're all behind him. We, his staff that is, know him quite well."

"I didn't imagine anyone knew him quite well," Nadia remarked.

"Few do, but he is far more of a generous man than he lets on," Ms. Cauthfield said with a smile. It seemed so wrong to Nadia; a chipper maidservant praising her master's generosity so sincerely? Had this been the same man, the one who had inherited from his sister - the one who had taken the family fortune, who had benefited from this warped system Lady Havenshire so despised? She began to wonder on whether she had too harshly judged him.

"He'll be here in just a moment; I need to check on things in the kitchen. It's been such a pleasure, m'lady," Ms. Cauthfield nodded, rushing off towards the doors at the rear of the long, tall chamber.

Nadia had to admit. Even the dining room chair felt so, unusually comfortable. Nonetheless, she steeled herself. He could present himself as fashionably and as bombastically as he wished; it would do little to change her mind on precisely what she felt about the nature of this entire arrangement her father had made. She wouldn't fall for it. Not for the fancy paintings or the stormy setting or the handsome face, or the mysterious nature of him, or--

"Announcing Lord Beckham, Duke of Berrewithe!" She couldn't stop herself from looking to the door - and there he was, wearing only a simple jacket, that same endless expression on his face; the one she had looked into, had almost gotten lost in, at the dinner party.

"You don't need to announce me, Ms. Cauthfield," Lord Beckham insisted with some manner of derision, as his maidservant emerged from behind him.

"Yes, I do! It's only proper," the woman insisted with a little self-satisfied snicker.

She denied it, so sternly, but... something about him, about Ms. Cauthfield, about all this, had begun to thaw that rigid iciness she had arrived carrying in her heart.

CHAPTER ELEVEN

"How is your braised beef, m'lady?" he asked plainly.

She wanted to tell him how it was. She wanted to tell him that the honeyed delicacy had crashed into her mouth with a ferocity of sweet and savory taste she had never anticipated, or yet experienced in so simple a dish. She wanted to tell him it tasted overwhelming; it tasted like nothing she had expected to taste, and that it had helped to set her free from the anger she carried with her after a week of suffering the rude and intolerable notions of a society bent against her. She wanted to tell him everything she had felt since she saw his manor, and since she saw what lived beneath it; a confusing mire that enticed her at the same time that it repulsed her, the majesty much like the beauty of northern England, which she both appreciated and deplored for what it represented. She wanted to tell him everything.

"It's fine," she said quietly, keeping her words sparse, and her emotions sparser. He didn't respond with words, but only a simple nod, seeming as out of place and as unsure of his feelings as she was, but she held out hope she could make it through this without exposing those feelings. Seated at the opposing end of the long dining hall, their words came not directly but as distant echoes reverberating along tall, vaulted ceilings.

She hadn't strayed yet from her original plan. She was halfway there; she need only finish her food, offer those same empty pleasantries as would be expected of her, thank her host, and leave. Then this week of contemplating and curiosity and hatred and of everything other confusing notion would end.

"It's rather lovely, isn't it," he asked, his voice that commanding and powerful tone she remembered, but feeling so... forced, so disingenuous. "The... sky," he said awkwardly. She regarded him closely, and began to think on a curious thought, one that struck hard at her pride. Had he been as anxious of this meeting of theirs as she had been? It wasn't something that would have troubled her before, but she could feel herself slipping.

"Yes," she responded coldly, and then silence. She devoured another exceptional bite of this braised beef, confident that she could report to Egan that whichever chef had crafted so divine a recipe deserved many times the credit he had given to the Havenshire home's kitchen staff. Knives and forks scraped against porcelain and teeth chewed quietly with mouths closed, but little else happened for a long and uncomfortable stretch of time.

"Your father is an honorable man," Lord Beckham said quaintly, making sure to clear out his throat before saying it, in the same stilted manner as his previous query. Something inside of Nadia flared up; perhaps that same, prideful part of hers that had brought words out from inside of her the first time they'd met. She'd always been willful, after all.

"Are these the manner of things you think it necessary or appropriate to say in the usual sort of courting ritual that women endure from rich dukes and barons?" she asked bluntly, surprised even at herself for having said it. She cleared her throat and an awkward silence followed. He shifted in his chair, watching her intently, and she wasn't certain her question would elicit an answer, and hoped that it would pass ignored, so that she could stick to her plot of remaining indifferent and leaving.

"To be perfectly honest, m'lady, I can't quite say I'm aware of the frivolities of the generic aristocratic courting ritual. If I was, I suppose this would probably be a far more successful and far more entertaining dinner between us," he responded rather casually, laughing softly, perhaps at himself. His response utterly infuriated Lady Havenshire... because it broke her composure, and she found herself grinning stupidly, just the same as he.

Damn it all, she thought to herself. The man bloody did it again; he made her feel something. He made her laugh, and smile.

"Are you certain? I think it'd be equivalently boring, myself," she snickered.

"Am I boring you? Blast it," Lord Beckham intoned sarcastically. "I suppose Lady Henrietta was wrong about me, after all. Quite a shock, right? As she's renowned for her truthfulness, and honesty, and for her ability to close her mouth, and all."

"You already made jokes at poor Lady Henrietta's expense, m'lord, you're not going to catch me with those again," Lady Havenshire teased playfully.

"Clever girl, she's on to my tricks," Lord Beckham quietly hissed. "Quickly, let's return to our discussion of precisely how boring I am. That had far greater possibilities."

"I've a better question for you," Nadia said, tapping her chin. "My father told me you were espousing some rather unorthodox thoughts to him, in your discussions about me. What, precisely, did you say to him that's got him thinking you're some sort of kindred spirit?" she hummed.

"Well, I expressed to him my feeling that you're a rather bizarre woman, and I'm a rather bizarre man, and us, being bizarre people, would do a wonderful job of terrifying the rest of the country together," he explained with joking pedantry, earning warm laughs from the lady, who nonetheless grew insistent.

"Tell the truth! I'm quite interested, now," Nadia smirked. Lord Beckham took a deep breath, glancing away.

"I'm certain that if I were to tell you, now, you'd take it as a simple ploy to whisk you away, marry you, and force you to have my children, or some other such lovely fantasy that I'm certain you're no stranger to," he admitted. "You'd think of my words as a ploy, and not as sincerity."

"Perhaps, but if you instead refuse, it's likely this conversation will die out the same as our previous conversation did, and I don't imagine that was much of a pleasant experience for either of us, was it?" Lady Havenshire admitted.

"What? I quite enjoy sitting in awkward silence with beautiful, intelligent women. It's good for one's soul," he joked.

"Then my speaking just now must have set you on the path to the devil, is that right?" Nadia returned with a wicked grin. Lord Beckham smiled, but collected himself and with gravity returned a genuine answer.

"Your father has an understanding of the rather unbecoming way in which our world treats women," he grudgingly admitted. "Nevertheless, he confessed to me his health has failed him, and that he hasn't the time to change all the world's hearts and all the world's minds, and instead hopes that before he passes he can marry you away. In our conversation, I admitted agreement with some of the methods of argument I'm certain he's heard from you, about how smart women ought to determine their own destinies. Those manner of things, you know," he said with a shrug.

"Not words a man says lightly in this sort of environment," Lady Havenshire offered. "I..." she, too, fought with herself about revealing what she had insisted she wouldn't about herself. "...I got a feeling from you, that night we met. You felt... different, from the sort of braying, selfish 'gentleman' that infects social circles. The sorts of men my friends all married. When I heard about your sister, I..."

"I loved my sister. A great deal. Leah had been my best friend, for most of my life," Lord Beckham interjected, overtaken by his emotion on the subject. "I... I believe, a part of what I feel, about you, about your father -- your situation... I want to pay for what I did to Leah."

"Have you spoken to your sister, of late? Does she hold it against you?" Lady Havenshire asked, confused as she was concerned.

"Leah... the death of father, the ruling of the magistrate, the estate... it all took her far too suddenly, and poisoned her heart. She left home, and I've not heard from her since," Lord Beckham recalled, voice full of melancholy. "I know... what you want, what your father wants. It's... not a marriage of love, but a marriage of... well, of convenience. One in which you bear my name, to carry on your line, and your wealth, and title, but... none of the burdens expected of a woman in a marriage. You need help, but want also to maintain your freedom. I feel that, if I... can't make up what happened to Leah, on my own. Perhaps I can do a small favor, to help unwrap this grand, terrible thing wrought upon the mindful women of this world."

The lord's speech ended and met with deafening silence. Her mind churning over the words, Lady Havenshire sat with her mouth slightly agape in surprise. She now felt only venom for herself for her presumptuous nature; for how quickly she had judged the lord in their last meeting. She lost her doubts in his sincerity; she saw in him something she had never truly expected to see.

Perhaps unlike the other gentlemen of England, when he said something... he meant it.

CHAPTER TWELVE

Today Lady Havenshire needed no servants to wake her; no vigorous and irritated rapping upon her door by Ms. Mulwray, excoriating the young woman for not rising before the sun did, nor needed she chiding summons from her father for spending a day in the bed. No, today instead Nadia rose at the first smell of early-morning dew wafting through her opened windows and between swaying, gossamer white curtains; before the sun had even set its eyes out across the fields, she smelled the new day, breathing its airs with aplomb, and rushed excitedly to face whatever it had to offer.

She could scarcely bring herself to admit it, but a little bit of excitement brimmed, bristled, burned in her heart; it's not a feeling she had ever had before, instead generally reserving her heart for feelings of contempt and questioning of men like Lord Beckham. But today, she awoke with new thoughts; new purposes. New dreams. Her cheek had met her pillow with her mind buzzing full of thoughts on the words he'd spoken; on the new side of this odd man she had seen set at the table, across from her; lamenting the loss of his sister, lamenting the way women must live in the cage that Nadia had spent her whole life trying to escape. Yet she tempered her excitement, as she rushed to the window to smell the scent of blooming flowers carried on gentle, cool breezes; she couldn't let herself get too carried away with the thoughts buzzing about in her mind.

Lord Beckham, confess as he might feelings of insecurity, or distaste with the nature of the life of 'gentlemen' in England - was nonetheless still a man, and she struggled to find it in herself to trust in his words or honesty. Though she reminded herself as dreams left and day began that she must remain wary, she couldn't stifle this sense of excitement. Today, Lord Beckham had agreed to visit the Havenshire manor - and here, in her own home, her own world, she would show him her own strengths; her convictions, her talents, and everything she'd learned. Thankfully, they'd be doing something together she had no questions of her talent for - riding. He had shown an interest in the horses' stables last he visited, hadn't he? Her mind ran away with thoughts of her, galloping freely atop Shadow's back, laughing into the wind as they raced together; for, she knew, every English gentleman knows how properly to tame a wild horse, does he not?

She had no way of explaining her feelings of excitement to herself; she'd not felt like she did, rising from bed today, since her youth; since days spent chattering with boys in their fathers' oversized jackets, gossiping and kissing one another on the cheek in the gardens outside the Emerys estate. As she breathed the fresh air, her cheeks burned a soft reddish hue, positively embarrassed by how odd she felt over this particular man. She remembered their first interaction and swallowed hard, stilling herself, trying once more to remind herself that this man had benefited from this system she so hated, even if he hated estrangement from his sister.

Such dark thoughts didn't become her, though, and she pulled her gown over her curves and thrust open the door to her bedroom, proudly striding into the corridor without and taking in the faint dim glow of sunlight through the hallways, and the tangy-sweet scent of lemon and essential oils, a fresh pronouncement that Ms. Mulwray had been up early preparing the house with the staff, cleaning and polishing every surface spotless before the sun took to its midday disposition. She dashed through the ornately-carved reliefs and pristine, soft carpets of the corridor outside her bedchamber, grinning as she had when she was an excited young girl, spiritedly jaunting through the Emerys gardens. Bouncing into her wardrobe, she offered a distinguishing eye to the collection of colored gowns and outfits - it would only be proper for a lady to ride on horseback wearing her finest gown, side-saddle, but Nadia grinned deviously, imagining the particular, witchy face Ms. Mulwray would scowl when she saw Nadia wearing her riding outfit. Nadia snatched her long, white jodhpurs from the shelf of the wardrobe, collecting her gloves and boots from shelves hidden behind flowing, white and lacy dresses and shawls in every manner of color imaginable. Her conspiratorial smile widened as she imagined her erstwhile suitor's curious expression when he saw Nadia dressed not for a leisurely gallop along the roadways, but for a quick and exciting trek across the Emerys holdings. She wondered, as she searched for her long navy-blue riding jacket, whether he would arrive wearing the same - just how serious, she pondered, was Lord Beckham in the matters equestrian? Another exciting question to find the answer to, soon.

"Lady Havenshire! M'lady!" Nadia's eyebrows bounced in surprise as she heard Ms. Mulwray's voice bounce through the hall outside, and the young noblewoman hurriedly fastened the buttons of her white riding blouse, before pulling her jacket overtop her curves and hurriedly wrapping her length of flowing hair into a single tail, bound with a pretty, silky white ribbon fetched from the drawers of the nearby vanity. She held her shoulders broad, her chest high, and her face brimmed with confident, curious satisfaction as she looked at her reflection, straightening down her jacket and pulling her boots taut and proper across her calves.

"Lady Haven-- Nadia!" Ms. Mulwray's voice grew louder as she stepped through the door to the expansive wardrobe; she gulped and stepped back in shock at seeing Nadia clad in her riding outfit. "C-certainly you're not intending to wear that to ride with Lord Beckham today! He's a proper gentleman, you know, and he'll certainly expect a woman he's sought to pursue to wear proper clothing," she scolded.

"Are you certain of that, Ms. Mulwray? How well do you know Lord Beckham, hmm?" Lady Havenshire teased, thinking on her past conversations with the unusual man, full of excitement at seeing just how he'll respond to a woman clad in the trappings of a professional, and not a dainty, helpless thing.

"M'lady, any man searching for a lovely lady to marry has no interest in seeing her dressed up in these sorts of... things," Ms. Mulwray spat.

"I think he'll like to see me in these things just fine," Lady Havenshire spat the word back with playful venom at the stern housekeeper. "You may find yourself surprised about Lord Beckham, Ms. Mulwray."

"Lady Havenshire, I've lived a life more than twice the length of yours, and I know only that if any charming gentleman searching the world for a suitor bore interest in a woman who so shamelessly paraded in the garb of a horse-jockey, he was rather reticent about it," Ms. Mulwray said judging, arms crossed atop her chest. "Think of your father for once, m'lady."

"I've thought plenty on him. Why do you think I went on that absurd dinner-date he pushed me in to, last night?" Nadia retorted, pulling her riding gloves over her fingers.

"And something quite positive came of it, didn't it? Perhaps you ought to listen to him more often," Ms. Mulwray heeded. Nadia hated to admit it, but... Ms. Mulwray and her father, in some small way, had been right, though perhaps not in the manner each of them expected. They had been right only on a technicality, with Lord Beckham proving far more a gentleman - the real, actual sort of gentleman - than she had expected. "You ought to make haste, m'lady - you wouldn't want to make him wait for too long, would you?"

"Lord Beckham's here already?" Nadia asked, stunned.

"Of course, m'lady - he's been waiting for you for nearly a half an hour!" Ms. Mulwray exclaimed. Nadia could answer only with surprised stutters; her heart throbbed at the thought that Lord Beckham, too, had spent the entire evening as vexed as she had been, contemplating the nature of their relationship; contemplating just what tomorrow would hold.

"I'll-- I, I should--" Nadia swallowed hard and, after another quick glance at her reflection, she rushed through the door, nearly tripping over her own feet in her dashing hubris, swirling around corners like a galloping steed, bounding down the stairs so quick she nearly fell onto her face when she skipped a whole step at the foot of them. She looked excitedly to the front door of the foyer - only to see Egan, standing attentive, arms crossed. Her heart throbbed briefly; had he waited too long? Had he grown bored and simply left? Had she lost her chance at meeting with him once more?

"Egan, where's Lord Beckham? Ms. Mulwray said--" she gasped, barely able to breathe. "Ms. Mulwray said that he'd come, has he gone? Has he left?" she demanded, her voice wobbly. Egan looked upon Nadia in utter bafflement, before gesturing to the couch near the stairwell - right in a blind spot, where Nadia's hurried gaze had failed to take notice of a man seated, patiently waiting. A stormy man with eyes deep as a swirling ocean.

"That sound in your voice, I quite enjoyed hearing it," Lord Beckham commented coyly as he rose, humbly approaching Lady Havenshire with a nod and a respectful look. "Was it just a hint of desperation, perhaps, that made it such a pleasant stew of a sound?"

"D-desperation? No, I'm just..." Nadia tried to collect herself. It had been a hint of desperation, though she would never admit it. "...I had hoped that I had no offended you by making you wait, is all." She looked at him, confused, seeing he had come to the manor wearing only his usual sort of breeches and jacket - dark and expensive, and he looked quite exceptionally handsome in them, as he had before, but... "...have you brought with you riding gear, m'lord? I had intended for us to ride together today, if you quite recall." An awkward silence fell as the duke glanced away, clearing his throat, and all at once an impish grin of glee spread across Lady Havenshire's face as she realized something quite salient.

"I suppose I had intended simply to ride in my usual manner of attire, m'lady," Lord Beckham conceded, clearing his throat.

"Don't you find that sort of riding rather uncomfortable? I had intended for us to ride rather seriously, after all," Lady Havenshire teased. "You'd find yourself much more comfortable, and safer, in the

101

proper attire... don't you think?" Lord Beckham grunted, once more nervously focusing his attention on the door.

"I think I shall do just fine as I am, m'lady," Lord Beckham bristled, and Nadia stifled a laugh. He couldn't ride quite at all, could he? Oh, she couldn't wait to savor the sight.

"Shall we make for the stables, then, m'lord?" Lady Havenshire asked with a devious, toying lilt to her voice. "I hope we can have quite an exhilarating ride before noontime."

"Erm... yes," Lord Beckham stated authoritatively, trying as best he could to play the role of the proper suitor and gentleman in front of the household staff. "Yes, of course, m'lady. Let's make for the stables." Lady Havenshire hid away a smirk and excitedly grasped the lord by the cuff of his jacket, leading him to the front door and throwing it open. The sun had begun to lift across the horizon, its yellowed morning light glance through the thick trees that covered the furthest fringes of the estate; with her tousle of wrapped hair bouncing behind her, Nadia giggled as she rushed along the side of the manor, down the stone path to the stables, where the horse's keepers had already begun their morning work, the horses grazing along the vast, grassy field, fenced and reserved just for them.

"Monsieur Therriault! We've come to take your finest steeds from you for the afternoon," Lady Havenshire announced proudly as she threw open the swinging door to the stables. Lord Beckham behind her seemed to feel utterly out of place, as he glanced at the horses still lazing about in their stalls. The horses' lead keeper, a whisper of a man in white working clothes with a dirtied beret atop his head, spoke with a Parisian accent thick as beaten cream.

"M'lady Nadia, always a pleasure to 'ave you in this part of the estate. Shadow 'as missed you so greatly in your years away from the estate," he crowed, his tone throaty. "She 'asn't let anyone ride her since you've been gone." The horse, which Nadia recognized as her beloved Shadow, whinnied as the door to its stall opened; the creature was quick to dart through the dirt and the straw to be at Nadia's side, and she soothed it with a gentle hand swaying across its bridle.

"I had expected no less a loyalty from her," Nadia smiled. "My sweet Shadow, the finest steed England's ever seen. Perhaps you'd like to take her riding for the day?" Nadia's smile turned devilish as she made the offer to Lord Beckham, who cleared his throat and stepped back.

"She seems to quite favor you, m'lady," he said, making an excuse. "Perhaps another horse for me? Shadow seems to have missed you upon her back."

"Oh, I'm certain any sort of proper gentleman could tame the wild heart of a girl like Shadow, could he not?" Lady Havenshire teased. "Come now, you'd not shrink away at such a chance to woo the heart of a wondrous woman such as I, would you?" she needled him. Monsieur Therriault looked on apprehensively as Lord Beckham sighed and accepted the churlish little challenge, moving alongside Shadow with his hands on the creature's back. Shadow whinnied in protest as Lord Beckham searched for some manner of mounting the creature, and it became quite immediately apparent that Lord Beckham in fact possessed practically no skill in the realm equestrian at all. Nadia's impish smile turned to stifled giggles as Lord Beckham awkwardly positioned himself at the animal's side, and then the other side; he finally, lopsidedly threw one leg atop the beast and nearly fell flat onto his back at that; when Shadow lifted her back in a roaring objection, Lord Beckham grasped one of the stable's support beams to stop himself from cracking his skull open upon the ground.

"And you've found me out," Lord Beckham admitted grudgingly as Nadia abandoned any pretense of subduing her laughter, instead letting it loose in long, girly snorts and chuckles.

"Just how long has it been since supreme gentleman Lord Marshall Beckham has rode upon a horse? Or even sat upon a horse?" Lady Havenshire asked with a smirk.

"If I quite recalled, perhaps I'd tell you," Lord Beckham sighed, giving her his own charming grin. She adored him in that moment; the gentleman who couldn't ride, certainly not nearly with the skill of Lady Havenshire, who quickly and skillfully mounted Shadow, the horse sniffing and snorting, clopping its hooves against the dirt in satisfaction at being reunited with her beloved owner.

"It's been that long, has it?" Lady Havenshire taunted, leading her horse towards the stable doors. "Monsieur Therriault, perhaps one of the older, slower steeds would be appropriate for Lord Beckham, yes?"

"I suppose I'm meant to take that as a clever manner of insult, m'lady," Lord Beckham quipped.

"Yes, you are, though you'd do well to remember I only tend to offer clever insults to men I rather like," Lady Havenshire admitted with a blush.

"I'll let him ride Pierre, then," Monsieur Therriault responded, corralling an older, dark-skinned horse from the rear of the stables.

"I've a warning for you, though, Lord Beckham," Lady Havenshire muttered through a grin.

"And what manner of warning is that?" an exasperated Lord Beckham asked as he awkwardly mounted the smaller, more complacent horse.

"I tend to be very competitive!" Lady Havenshire exclaimed as she gave her horse a quiet whistle, the animal setting off from the stable doors with a sudden whinny and a loud flourish. "Try to keep up!" Lady Havenshire called back to him with a laugh.

CHAPTER THIRTEEN

Fast - air rushing, breeze blowing, trees swaying; their colors a stunning, vibrant array of blazing autumn oranges, browns, and rich, sunny yellows. Clouds gathered dark at the edges of a pristine sky as Shadow's hooves clamped and smashed and clobbered cobblestones and fallen leaves, until Lady Havenshire, laughing at the freedom and the joy of being atop her horse's back once again, with all the world before her to traipse upon as she saw fit, drew her horse's reigns off-road and into the tall, roiling grasses near the fringes of the Emerys estate.

Nothing in the world felt quite like the freedom of riding upon Shadow's back - she'd rode steeds in other countries, she'd rode boats upon the open ocean; but to Nadia, even the flight of birds had little on the one thing she loved her home for, the joy of riding across fields, cutting through forests, leaping over streams, with the worries of the world behind her and nothing but her dreams to contain her. She laughed away the worry; she laughed away thoughts of her father, thoughts of the estate; the caging burdens of life that'd fallen once more onto her shoulders when she'd returned to England. To all of it she simply laughed and drove Shadow along, swerving through weeds; hooves clopping through a dirt field, past an abandoned farmhouse, its thatched roof having rotted away and its stone foundation crumbling like some manner of ancient, collapsed Roman bathhouse.

Only after so joyously trotting upon Shadow for so long, longer than she could care to remember, well into the waning moments of the morning, did Lady Havenshire finally remember that she had not galloped alone out onto the moors; worse yet she remembered that the curious man to whom she'd found herself oddly attracted was not, in fact, any good at all with horses. She looked back in worry from where she'd come and - not surprisingly - saw no sign at all of Lord Beckham upon the aging, deep-brown horse, Pierre. The smile washed from her expression, replaced with momentary worry; she could hear little across the fields save for the soft sway of grass and leaves, tossed about by the gentle breeze. She searched the autumn-tinted trees and their bouncing leaves; she searched the dead farm field, and saw nor heard a single sign of the poor man. She bit her lip, sudden worry shocking her, and she began to scold herself for so thoughtlessly abandoning Lord Beckham. Is he okay, she wondered? Worse yet, has he turned from me for my impetuousness? Perhaps, she thought, she should have listened to Ms. Mulwray; perhaps, just this once, she had been right. Things would have gone so much better, simpler, had Nadia rode quaintly side-saddle while Lord Beckham took his time on Pierre. If only...

Suddenly, a faint gallop struck Nadia's ear, and like an alerted hawk her senses shot towards the edge of the trees. There, what she saw tilted her worrisome frown into a slow, warm smile; trotting like a mountain-man upon an overburdened ass, Lord Beckham emerged from one of Emerys' forests, gripping onto Pierre's reigns with all the strength and adroitness he could manage. She stifled another chuckle, as the horse stumbled and jaunted at a pace that could only be described as embarrassing. He looked up, his eyes crossed with an expression not unlike that of a child balancing precariously upon a tightrope, his gaze stricken with awed fear at the pace of the beast beneath him.

"The forest was that dangerous, was it?" Lady Havenshire called across the field to Lord Beckham; the sound startled the poor man, whose grip on the horse's reins tightened. Pierre appeared to respond to Lady Havenshire's voice, perhaps taking the words as a challenge. The horse picked up speed and began bounding towards Nadia and Shadow, and Lord Beckham's gaze shifted from terrified to... well, to even more terrified, as the horse threatened to quite summarily throw the poor lord off of his back with each bucking burst of speed.

"This blasted creature--" Lord Beckham howled, bouncing side-side on Pierre's back as the beast trotted across the dead field. "How do you tell it to slow down?!"

"Slow down? You could walk faster than Pierre is carrying you!" Nadia laughed uproariously.

"Perhaps I sh-should!" Lord Beckham responded, squeezing the reins tightly as Pierre finally began to slow, clearly exhausted by carrying the lord across the field. With a quiet yip Nadia led Shadow along the field to meet Lord Beckham; she skillfully led Shadow to a quick, light-hoof trot in a wide circle around Pierre, who snorted and trotted while Lady Havenshire rode in a circle around the man.

"Such a skilled rider you are," Lady Havenshire grinned.

"I'm beginning to see just why your father feels you utterly unmarriageable, m'lady," Lord Beckham teased. Pierre stepped to a stop in the middle of the field and rather unceremoniously plopped onto the mud, laying down with a yawn, leaving Lord Beckham's boots scuffed with layers of the mud. Lady Havenshire laughed, petting her hand along Shadow's bridle.

"Is that so? Do you think me utterly unmarriageable, then,

m'lord? Must a woman stand before you in fear of sundering her beauty, pleading with you to teach her the ways of the beasts of wild, before you find her agreeable to a marriage, m'lord?" Lady Havenshire's voice grew thick with derisive sarcasm as she trotted closer, her circle around lazy Pierre narrowing. Lord Beckham pulled himself from the lazy animal's back, dusting away the dirt and the leaves clung to his jacket from the slow trip through the autumn forest, exhaling deeply. She could see the humble smile forming on the charming gentleman's lips and she bit her own, her cheeks reddening as she teased him. He liked it, she thought... and so did she.

"For me, a woman's skill upon the back of a steed means comparatively little, though I must say that the outfit you're wearing is itself rather... well, an interesting choice for an afternoon spent with a man of my status," Lord Beckham chided her in a deadpan, joking manner; she feigned offense.

"Ms. Mulwray said you would say just that very thing, so you've certainly won her vote of approval for taking my hand in marriage," she joked.

"And what, pray tell, have you gotten into your head, m'lady, to convince you I have any interest in taking your hand, then?" Lord Beckham retorted.

"It certainly couldn't be the manner in which you invited me into your domain, and made me smile once again, just as we had at that dreadful dinner, before... well, before, you know," Nadia stated cheekily, before the memory of Lord Beckham's sister again cast clouds across their exchange. She tried to brighten the mood, offering Lord Beckham a hand to hoist him up out of the mud. He regarded her suspiciously, and instead squished his way free of the mire, dusting off his boots with a humph.

"Trees are... a fair bit sparser, on my land, and there are certainly fewer forests to be found," Lord Beckham mentioned, glancing at the thick tree line they had both precariously trotted their way through.

"Emerys has long had some of the finest forests and hunting grounds in all of northern England," Nadia explained. "Father had little interest in attracting hunters, and tore down many of the cabins and hunting lodges my grandfather and his fathers had used to draw renters and trappers out this way. I always appreciated the forests more for days like today... when the autumn comes, and the colors sweep across the leaves, and the breezes kick them around... as a child, I also enjoyed the trees for climbing, and playing," she recalled with an evil little grin. "Poor mother, she'd go searching the moors for me, always winding up ruining one of her finest dresses, trudging through the mud and the branches looking for me."

"You would have gotten along rather terrifically with Leah," Lord Beckham laughed. He tried various calls and cries and snorts and sounds to lure Pierre out of the muddy morass he'd decided to lay in, but the stubborn old horse had little interest in the man or his antics.

"Did she too enjoy leading your mother wildly about the estate?" Nadia chuckled, leading Shadow into the muddy field and with a few deft motions and noises, she'd managed to coax Pierre whinnying to his hooves. She beamed at Lord Beckham, who shrugged in defeat.

"I tried," he said with a frown. "I suppose you're quite right. I'm not much a gentleman, am I?"

"Are you perhaps throwing out a line in hopes of finding a

compliment on the other end? That's certainly a pitiable thing for a gentleman to do," Lady Havenshire chided.

"Considering my current predicament, I think I've made myself look quite pitiable already," he quipped back, looking down at the mud now staining his breeches. Nadia giggled, shaking her head.

"Pitiable? Perhaps, though poor Pierre's the one who laid down in the stuff," Nadia snickered. "You didn't answer me... about your sister," Nadia's voice fell to a curious murmur; Lord Beckham sighed, glancing away, and Nadia's own expression grew worrisome. "I hope I don't... conjure, poor thoughts, with such a subject."

"Thoughts of Leah are rarely poor, m'lady, as she's one of the most capable and amazing people I've met - woman or man," Lord Beckham said resoundingly. "I have... a lot to make up for, in life, for the way she was... treated."

"Have... you ever thought, of trying to find her? Sending her a letter? It appears you care for her deeply, Marshall, and... I think she may have cared deeply for you, too," Nadia said, leaping down from Shadow's back to stand close to the duke. He looked away, vexed again with doubt; that same doubt, creeping back, and Nadia tried to plead silently with him not to shut her out.

"I doubt very much Leah wants to hear from anyone, wherever she's gone, and I can't rightly blame her, m'lady. I've got a lot to repent for," Lord Beckham responded, and Lady Havenshire could see the storm brewing in his eyes as dark shadows fell across the both of them.

Unfortunately, the storm in Lord Beckham's soul was not the only storm brewing at that particular moment in time. As Nadia drew closer, trying to comfort the sullen duke, a loud thunderclap shattered their moment together; startled, the two nobles looked to the sky, only noticing all too late that a thunderstorm had darkened the moors and forests of the Emerys estate. Nadia hastily glanced across the fields - they had spent all morning riding, into the afternoon, and had ranged too far for the two of them to make it back safe to the manor in time.

"The storm doesn't seem interested in waiting for us to complete this particular conversation," Lord Beckham said, his voice once again strong, alluring; and now, full of duty, as he searched for a resolution to their particular situation. A slow panic set into Nadia's mind; she hadn't realized just how far they had ranged, nor had she been paying attention to the weather, and she quietly cursed herself.

"I'm... sorry, I'm not certain that Pierre can make it terribly far in heavy rains," she said, voice warbling. Lord Beckham comforted Nadia's fear, stroking her tied-back tail of flowing hair as he quickly thought on a decision; another thunderclap echoed overhead.

"You spoke of your father tearing down the hunting lodges and cabins, though - generally, estates like these have gamesman or warden cabins - do you remember any, possibly still standing, out in the woods?" Lord Beckham said. "I'd presume they'd be located... back, the route we came, in the deepest part of the forest."

"Y-yes!" Nadia recalled. "I... I don't think Father has had it torn down since last I lived on the estate, but a gamekeeper's cabin once laid in the heart of the forest's edge here, if we can--" a loud crash of thunder, a flash of lightning, and a light, dewy misting of rain fell down upon them all at once, and with each movement intent, Lord Beckham grasped Pierre's bridle; the horse whinnied, and he set Lady Havenshire upon her steed with great, effusive strength.

"We must be hasty, ride ahead of the storm as best we can," he insisted. Nadia blinked at the sudden strength shown by the man, but she had little time to contemplate now, driving Shadow back into the darkness of the forest as the lightning and thunder nipped at the horse's hooves.

CHAPTER FOURTEEN

"Here!"

She heard his voice pierce through the waves of rain falling overhead; cascading, wet waves, sheets of the stuff now coating her, soaking through her thin riding jacket. She shivered as Shadow trotted and whinnied in protest, feeling the fear and the chill running down Nadia's back. Lord Beckham's cry felt like utter providence; she pulled back on the reins of her steed, who took off through the thickets and blanket of fallen leaves into the forest like an arrow plunging to its target. Nadia held close, a shiver rocking her frame as she held on tight, hearing only the soft patter of her shocked pulse reacting to the cold. Lord Beckham had gone ahead in search of the cabin; she remembered it from her childhood, and the grumpy, strange man who had lived out in the woods; one bulging eye, clad always in clumsily-sewn furs, occasionally dragging reams of sliced venison in a cart for her father to serve during dinner banquets.

"M'lady?" she heard him cry out in concern as another thunderous crack struck the sky, lightning creasing through coal-gray clouds. She raised her hoarse voice to assure him, but she could speak barely above a whisper, the cold soaking through into her bones. A painful eternity passed before they arrived at a small clearing, Shadow hopping over a fallen, rotted log and a handful of gnarled, aged branches as she saw him there in the doorway; her peculiar, but strong, savior. Her breath ragged she gripped tightly to Shadow as the horse brought her alongside Pierre, who had already decided to take a rest in the mud again, rain splattering against the creature's back.

"M'lady, I'm begging your pardon, but you look quite dreadful," Lord Beckham joked as her arm across his shoulders and hoisted the soaked, cold, tired woman off of her horse's back. The position brought to her pained memories of her father, struggling to make it up the stairs, and she shook her soaked dreams loose and pulled herself up proudly, not willing to let a man do her walking for her.

"I... I'll be just f-fine," her lips chattered at the cold along her skin, and she shivered her way through puddles of mud and overgrown, marshy grasses, her boots now sloshing as water and mud snuck through the leather and clung to her stockings. Her legs shaky, she nearly lost her balance in the mire - Lord Beckham was quick to grasp and steady her, though he kept his distance, not wanting to patronize the proud woman with the offer of unnecessary help. She smiled glibly, not sure if he had come to recognize her as an equal quite yet... but it was a nice step.

"I'm c-cold," she shuddered as she pulled open to the door to the cabin. Lord Beckham saw her in and surprise swept her features at how pristinely preserved the place appeared; she had utterly forgotten it even existed after the gamekeeper passed years ago, and she had thought the same of her father; and perhaps he had. But aside from dust clung to the trophy heads of elk and moose and deer and exotic manners of beast arrayed along the walls, the cabin felt positively homey; a fireplace sat unused, dried logs adjacent to the stone mantle, a writing desk off to one corner; a rather Spartan bed in a simple frame with white, dusty sheets in one corner; a velvety couch set opposite the fireplace, cushions overstuffed with goose feathers. Nadia took stilted steps inside as Lord Beckham pulled the door shut behind them, the rain pattering loudly against the roof; she could spot no leaks, the cabin again defying every expectation, as even the family manor itself had run afoul of various holes in the roof over the years.

"M'lady, please," Lord Beckham pointed her to the couch, his movements and voice and everything about him, so full of that duty. She had not yet seen him like this, so dedicated; he had something he needed to accomplish, and he moved with haste and attention to do just what he needed to do. She appreciated it silently, her teeth chattering, her hair streaming with moisture; she wrung her messy ponytail out to draw some of the moisture away from her head, though it did little to abate the shiver shocking her spine. Lord Beckham grasped the wrought-iron fire poker at the mantle and used it to claw cobwebs and sheets of dust from the fireplace, rolling over the dried-out wooden logs from the pile nearby and throwing them into the stone chamber, searching for any manner of match or flint with which to ignite the objects.

"It's... I didn't r... remember, how cold it could get in r-rainstorms, here," Lady Havenshire said, shuddering; Lord Beckham's face, vexed in concern, turned to the woman; noticing her shivers hadn't calmed, he approached her and grasped the shoulders of her soaked jacket. He very carefully tugged at the garment, taking great care not to act in a manner unbecoming of her own autonomy; he slid the soaked jacket down her body, off of her arms, hanging it atop one of the bedposts, droplets of water flowing freely from the cloth, so saturated with rain that it quickly created a puddle beneath it.

"The rain makes it far worse, m'lady, as do wet garments

swimming atop your skin," he murmured to her. She heard a soft shuffling and turned to see the duke removing his own heavy jacket - it fared far better in the rain, its leathery surface having deflected much of the rainwater, its interior lined with furs and stuffed comfortably; she could feel the jacket's warmth and squirmed as he placed the garment across her shoulders. It was far too large for her, of course, but the extra size only made it all the warmer and more comforting.

"I'm... I d-don't think I've ever seen a j-jacket, like this one," Nadia chattered out, smiling meekly as her skin flushed from a deep pale to a light, lively pink.

"The weather on the moors of Berrewithe has a tendency to get rather unpleasant as autumn and winter approach, particularly at the manor and in the hills beyond," Lord Beckham said, eyes scanning the mantle for something to finish his fire-tending task with. She watched him in quiet awe - now, without his jacket, she got to see more than she had ever gotten to see before, his white silk undershirt clung to Lord Beckham's body... a body she quickly came to appreciate. A chiseled frame lay beneath the garb, his chest broad and virile; his arms powerful, his skin a rich, deep and alluring tone, his damp hair thrown to one side of his alluring face as he searched the cabin for a flint to strike. She gasped gently on seeing him, more impressed by a man than she perhaps ever had been, though that little impish voice inside of her reminded her to remain steady. Not to get carried away. He was still a man, a privileged man, even with that... tempting body, and those eyes, and his powerful voice...

"Ah," he finally exclaimed in satisfaction, discovering a small flint and tinder in a box upon the mantle. "Now, let us hope we're fortunate enough that years of mold and damp rains haven't fouled the wood, and that rust hasn't claimed the fire steel," Lord Beckham commented quietly as he kneeled before the fireplace. Lady Havenshire found herself drawn curiously to his back, as if in a trance; she couldn't stop looking at those chiseled lines of strength and masculinity drawn across his back, visible through his wet shirt. She swallowed hard, adoring the sight of him; still so unsure of what she'd found in him, but so wanting. She heard the repetitive click-click of a rigid chert struck against the small piece of steel; as she came around the couch she saw a small, flashing spark kicked towards the dried-out wood. He repeated the motion as she watched, the chill lifted from her back, her cheeks now burnished a bright tone as she watched his every movement. She took a ragged breath - the sound haggard not from the cold now, but from the adrenaline-rush of emotions in her warmed veins, so enticed by a man who so selflessly helped her from the cool touch of the rushing rains.

With a quiet roar a fire kicked up from the meet of sparks and log, and the flames spread quick, until a warming glow flowed outward and through the cabin, coating both of its inhabitants with an orange-tint glow. Her eyes flashed alight and she felt the warmth begin to cascade over her. Lord Beckham turned, faced her and smiled, shrugging.

"I suppose that... worked, did it not, m'lady?" he asked, a boyish sort of humble charm to his words. She remained silent; she found it hard, in fact, to speak, or to think; she had so utterly been taken by her interest in him that it reduced her to something of a simpering little girl.

"I..." she tried; he stepped closer, and she could smell his scent, feel his warmth; his broad chest before her, she felt the need to press her cheek to it, to hear his heart beating, to know he was flesh and blood and man like all the others, and not some manner of wild dream her imaginative mind had conjured up to fill her fantasies.

"The fire should help... you've not caught some manner of malady out in the cold, have you, m'lady?" he asked, worriedly. She bit her bottom lip, her shoulders shaking. "M'lady, I..." she silenced his concerned words by pressing her fingers suddenly to his shirt; he recoiled at first, and she could tell that a part of him still felt so averse to a woman's touch. Such a mystery was he; she had divined some terrible thing had befallen him in the past, to hurt his heart so much as it was; she felt all at once compelled to heal him, as best she could.

"L... Lord Beckham," she whispered, her words unsteady as she toyed with the buttons on his shirt.

"M'lady, I..." he said strenuously, glancing to the dingy window, watching the rain fall.

"W... what happened?... d... do you not... like the touch, of... of a woman..." she said. "Your shirt is... is soaked, you must be q... quite cold..."

"I'm n... I'm fine, I ju..." his voice trailed away; his expression grew both enthralled, and pained, as if some great hesitation stewed beneath his skin, forcing him to shudder, full of fear. "I... I deeply, deeply desire the touch of a w... a woman, of you, but I... I'm not worth, I'm not-- I'm not as much of a man, a gentleman, as you think I am."

"Lord Beckham..." she whispered.

"Marshall," he insisted quietly, hesitantly opening his arms and gently, so gently, pulling her closer.

"Marshall, why... why do you think you're... undeserving?" she queried, her voice such a faint whisper; heedless she carefully parted the top button, the sight of his chest causing her to shiver a very, very different sort of shiver than those sent down her spine by the piercing cold.

"I... I loved a woman once, m'lady," he started.

"Nadia... please, Nadia," she insisted, smiling weakly as she undid the second button; with each new inch of him that came into her sight she felt her heart pump harder.

"Nadia, I once loved a woman... she left me alone, and I've... I've never known a love like the one she and I shared, and I fear I never will, but..."

"...but...?" Nadia asked, fingers shaking uncontrollably. He needed no more impetus; as the rain roared above and around and the thunder cracked in the distance he pressed his lips to hers and a fire erupted, hotter than the one behind them; hotter than anything she could have imagined. Their hearts thumped passionately together and she began furiously to undo the buttons, one after another after another, her hands hungry for his skin, massaging his muscles, his olive-toned skin; she gasped as their kiss ended, but it did so for only a second, his hands gripping her back and holding her close, his jacket falling down her back as they kissed and kissed, kissed the cold away; kissed away pained memories and all the fears that had divided them since that night where the sparks began to fly between them.

CHAPTER FIFTEEN

She moaned, her voice quivering, quaking uncontrollably as he laid her against the plush cushions of the dusty couch; his jacket upon the floor, he worked impatiently to pull one button free, and then another; her gasps filled the air as he took her so completely. He silenced her sounds by kissing her again, pulling button from button so teasingly and painfully slow; she wanted it faster, faster, because every part of her body screamed out for him as he peeled her sleeves away. He grunted, frustrated to find a sleek white bustier clung to her body beneath the shirt; she pressed a coy finger to his lips and grinned devilishly, her wet body warmed by the touch of the fireplace and the hungry touch of the man before her as she reached behind her, arching her back away from the couch and grasping the zipper at her back, letting it slide slowly down until the garment felt loose against her petite frame and her pretty young curves. His hands shook and hesitated; he wanted to see her, her milky skin and her pretty face and her flowing hair and everything about her, but a fear struck him, as it did so often when it came to women, and she saw him freeze and think twice as he grasped at her loose undergarment. She reassured Marshall with a gentle touch to his wrists, guiding his hands along, pulling the bustier away and laying it on the floor beside them. Her heart thumped faster and harder as the warmth of the fire met her bare breasts, the pretty pink dollops of sugary nipple flesh stiff as she felt him grasp her chest and feel her, his eyes filled with a desire she had never seen in him; free and full, just as her own had been. She tugged at the shirt laying across his shoulders the buttons unfastened, and he quickly threw the silky white top away, bearing the full breadth of his chest, his arms; his taut abs and his rock-hard flesh quaking atop her body.

Ravenous and uncaged he buried his lips into her neck, devouring her with a flurry of starved kisses along her jawline, to her neck, down her chest; he paid attention to every inch of her sweet and sugar-white skin, swirling his tongue hotly across her, lapping up the dew of the rainstorm with each kiss, replacing the soaked droplets with furious kisses and deep, desirous moans against her. He pressed her wrists down beside her, and while she cherished her freedom, the only thing that made her feel even freer than her liberated ideals was the sensation of a strong man giving her everything she wanted, even without the need to speak; to surrender herself to the pleasure his lips and his tongue and his strong frame had to offer to her. He gripped her wrists tightly and grew ravenous, keeping her pinned as her back pressed so that her body could savor every kiss, her lungs shaking with lusty moans with each inch of her the lord claimed.

"Marshall, I've... I've never felt like this, nothing like this, before, with anyone," she admitted sheepishly, her cheeks a blistering pink-red as she spread her legs, hastily tugging at the zippers of her boots. He helped her to undo each foot and pulled them from her legs, removing her boots and stockings with a slow, slow pull. She could see him trembling hard, his hands jittering with all the pent-up emotion, the need, the desire. "I d... don't, don't know how to t... tell you, but..." she felt a lump in her throat; his hands rolled comforting along her arms until they came to her shoulders; he massaged them gently and laid close to her, their lips meeting in a twining passion for another long, intense kiss, their tongues dancing together, their eyes meeting, their hearts pounding; she felt his strong chest pressed against hers and she shivered, her nipple stiff against his puissant flesh.

"Anything, anything you want to say, anything you want - in all the world, Nadia," he whispered to her, his kisses moving along her cheek and meeting her earlobe, which he worshiped with an animalistic hunger, nipping at her sensitive skin as the words came tumbling from her wanting lips.

"I-I've never b-been, never been intimate with a man, before," she admitted, shaking hard beneath him, sinking into the couch, fearful her inexperience would foul the tense desire built between the two of them. She looked to him, concern crossing her eyes, and he dispelled all her worries with a kiss to her lips, one that melted away all that ice and blew away the smoky cloak of fear in her body.

"I'll do anything I can to make you feel like the goddess you are, Nadia," he promised, kisses raining along her neck; she swooned with a quiet, melodic breath as she felt him kiss her again and again, along her breasts, down to her stomach; his kisses moved further, and further, until he began to tug gently at her leggings with his teeth and hands slipped into her waistline. Her hips lifted to help him, and for all the strength that Nadia possessed, all of her firebrand independence, when he began to rain kisses across her supple thighs, grasping at her hips and worshiping upon her altar with whispered words of desire, she melted utterly, forgetting about everything; about her father, about her future, about the estate; he made it all seem like a long-distant nightmare, one she'll never have to face again with him there.

"P... please, Marshall, do... don't stop, don't ever stop," she pleaded with quivering, breathy words. Her body nude before him, something she had never felt comfortable doing with any man, she couldn't control the quaking along her spine or the moans beginning to cascade from between her lips. His kisses drew closer and closer to the most sensitive part of her, her folds flush and warm and damp; his tongue worked skillfully to tease at her thighs, hotter and hotter and faster, until she felt him lavishing praise upon her feminine slit, tongue swirling up one side and down the other, devouring in worship her hot nectar and pleasing her flushed femme bead with skilled licks and laps as he watched her with those deep and entrancing eyes. She began to cry out hungrily, loudly; her hips pressed out, wanting more, and more, and when she felt his warm tongue slip inside of her and feast upon her sweet depths, her eyes opened wide and she couldn't stop herself from erupting into a shaky moan, like the shrill sound of a songbird whistling over the moors. Her shivering fingers wrapped between his hair and squeezed his scalp and she couldn't even feel anything except how good it was; she couldn't imagine anything except him, for the rest of her life, worshiping her, making her feel like nothing in the entire world ever had.

"M-Marshall!" she managed to put the syllables of his name together, before those sweet swooning moans began falling from her lips again, wordless melds of impassioned sounds; he drew his tongue warmly across her most sensitive depths, licking along her front wall, twirling at her pearly clit until she could scarcely take it anymore. She felt an erupting sensation sizzling into her stomach, filling her every limb with a heavenly, tingling warmth, warmer than any coat or fireplace or anything could ever make her. Waves of desire filled every inch of her and she tugged at his hair and moaned his name over and over again as he pleasured her deftly and quickly and skillfully.

As the waves of intense pleasure filled her, he crawled atop her body, covering her in sweet kisses from her stomach to her neck, and reality snapped back into place as she watched him closely; she wanted more, more, and she coaxed him with a frustrated little moan and a wiggle of her hips against his body. With that stormy, authoritative tone in his voice he silenced her protests, pressing his hips against hers.

"Nadia," he murmured, kissing between every word. "I want... you, I want you like... this feeling, so intense, I can't put it to words," he admitted, kissing along her lips and down the side of her neck. She grasped at his waistline, and he unlatched his belt, loosening his breeches and letting them fall to his knees. His thick, throbbing masculine length erupted from beneath his pants, and he took a deep breath, kissing her neck gently as he led his shaft softly against her sweet folds, massaging its tip against her clit; he shuddered against her, letting out growling, feral moans as he grasped the base and gently, so gently pressed it inside of her depths, inch by slow, throbbing inch; her eyes wide and her words lifted skyward Nadia gasped and shrieked in pleasure, her nails digging deep into his back and begging for him to take her.

"M-Marshall, it f... feels so, d-divine," she whispered, raking her nails along his back. He obliged those silent pleadings, pressing harder, deeper, until she felt him feel her completely, stretching her sensitive opening; her nerves screamed, thunderbolts louder than any ravaging the cabin in the storm outside, rocketed along her limbs; she shuddered beneath him, and she felt that same, climactic and explosive pleasure fill her from her stomach through her chest, her body tensing, her depths tightening around his length as she clasped tight around his whole body like a vise. And yet when he continued to push, his shaft pressing in, and out, and in and out, she quaked like she never had; god, it was even better than she imagined it could be, and nothing in the entire world mattered at all except for their endless, powerful lust.

"I'm... god, you're unbelievable," Marshall murmured into her ear as he took a throbbing, enticing rhythm, entering her hard, steady, but always gentle to take care of her sweet, virginal body. She held on to him tight, letting him take her, each thrust feeling heavenly. He squeezed and kissed her deeply, his breath teasing her skin, growing faster and hotter with each deep, powerful thrust. She felt herself building to a new, explosive climax, like nothing she had felt ever before, her breaths deeper and faster as the fire flashed and crackled, its light coating their body now with sweat, the heat of their lovemaking washing away the damp cool of the rain. She couldn't speak, she couldn't do anything except think on how perfect this experience was; he, too, began to lose control, and she felt his thrusts grow ragged and wild and his hands shake as he grasped and squeezed her breasts and her hips and every part of her, with each of his touches only making her hotter and hotter.

The lightning crackled and flashed through the window, electric-blue light raking across their skin as Marshall thrust deep and hard, filling her to his hilt; he cried out her name like no sound she had ever heard, and she sung his own as she felt her body fill with a powerful thrum of pleasure, shaking her to her very core as she reached her tingling, perfect climax. She felt his throbbing length inside of her explode with hot, pleasurable waves of his release pumping hot and moist against her inviting feminine depths. She held him close and he, her, as they met their perfect finish together, their breaths twining and their eyes looking into one another adoringly as this impeccable moment passed.

She smiled weakly at him, unable to say anything; she only kissed, and kissed his lips, as he lay atop her, barely able to breathe. He laid his head against her chest, and he could certainly hear the constant, powerful pound of her heart, rocked by something she had never experience before.

She began to ponder as they lay together, basking in their joined glow, if this could be what love felt like; if she had stumbled into the woods and come upon something she couldn't have ever imagined.

"Marshall..." she said, breathlessly. He answered with a kiss, a comforting kiss; a kiss comforting unlike any she'd ever had before. She realized she had never wanted a gentleman; she had never wanted a boy. She had wanted Marshall.

CHAPTER SIXTEEN

The storm had begun to rumble to a close, just as the old logs burned out their last few sparking embers; and by that time, Lord Beckham and Lady Havenshire had spent the entirety of the afternoon, into the beginning of the evening, simply laying together; enjoying the feeling of warmth their bodies gave one another. They had slipped into a much-needed nap together, and Lord Beckham's eyes opened from sweet reverie only a few moments after they had drifted into slumber. Lady Havenshire tossed in her sleep, her nude body shuddering; Lord Beckham grasped his coat, pulling it gently atop the two of them, which seemed to calm her raucous tossing and comfort her. He exhaled deeply, so taken with how perfect things had gone today between the two of them.

A few subsiding thunderclaps filled the air, though none loud enough to wake Nadia from her rest; and for that, the lord was thankful, as he thought after such an afternoon, she needed her sleep. He, on the other hand, could scarcely still the hot, fast pounding of his heart; he had again felt the touch of a woman, a woman who seemed so deeply to care for him, and had begun to wonder if he had found something he thought he never could again - true love, like he had with Anna. He smiled quietly to himself as he wrapped an arm around Lady Havenshire, holding her close to his sweat-tinged chest; he exhaled into her ear, silently whispering into her dreams, though he had no way of knowing if she'd ever hear his coy admissions, or simply write them off as the murmurings of her own, fevered dreams.

"I think I love you, Nadia... I didn't know if I could ever love again, but... something in my heart, beats just for you," he whispered, closing his eyes. He felt an ethereal comfort fall upon his shoulder; she wriggled in his grasp, cuddling closer against the duke's body, and he soon fell off the edge of consciousness and into deep dreaming.

And what he saw hadn't changed.

Dreams took him to a place far in the past, far from the estate. The rumble of the thunder and the fall of the rain through the forest had brought his mind back to dark places, even if he hadn't noticed it. As the rain fell overhead, it fell in Lord Beckham's dreams; he saw her, again; the face he had hoped to never see again. Anna - his love, the woman who had left him on the day of their wedding. He found a letter from her atop his desk, after the rainstorm began to fall over the wedding. The storm raging outside of the cabin, as Lord Beckham lay in restless sleep, brought his mind back to that day; to the letter that had so shattered him for so long.

I can't simply remain with a man as complacent as thee, it had said. Anna always had a method of cutting at Lord Beckham's heart, and she would, so often, no matter how much love he heaped upon her. You'll never be a man capable of having me. A woman needs something more than satisfaction. The Lord Timonere can offer me so much more than that.

He had never expected it - for her to leave him, so coldly. Outside of the reverie Lord Beckham turned, brow coated in sweat; he breathed hard, distressed, as the thunderstorm crackled in his memories; as the dreams ravaged him with pain at the loss. She had told him he'd never be good enough for a true woman, and he had kept loving her.

A crack of thunder rattled the cabin and Lord Beckham shot up from sleep, awoken by the sound, the sting of Anna's letter still fresh in his memory. Startled awake, Nadia's expression, full of concern, turned to her lover.

"Marshall? What's bothering you?" she asked, her voice a wobbly whisper, her eyes vexed in worry. He looked away, to the fireplace; he watched those last few embers crackle and die away, struggling in search of an answer to calm her.

"There's no need to worry, Nadia," he insisted, leaning down to kiss her on the lips. With that kiss, her worries ebbed away and she snuggled in comfort beneath the coat again, wrapping her hand around the duke's waist.

But something did quite deeply, profoundly worry him. His mind alight, he breathed deep, listening to the rain. It had slowed, and the thunder had faded, but each fallen raindrop reminded him of that day. Each patter brought him back to rain falling upon benches; sorrow-filled revelers gathered beneath the mansion's arcade, watching as the bouquet of flowers the lord had ordered for his bride lay soaked, drowned in the rain.

He had let Anna down. He could never make a woman happy - not with his face, or his body, or the way he talked. A woman wanted drive; a woman wanted ambition, a woman wanted everything he wasn't.

He sat, and he thought. How did he know he wouldn't let Nadia down, too?

The dreams dwelt, no matter how he tried to push them away. The thought of that letter - of the lovely times he'd had with Anna. Ms. Cauthfield had never been one to mince words on her feelings about

Anna - she saw the woman as a scheming, social climber, who had never truly cared for Lord Beckham but only for the Berrewithe estate and the position it earned her. But whether that had been true or not, Marshall had truly loved her - as cruel and capricious as she could be, he had stayed by her, forgiven her; he had accepted her for her. Like Nadia, her father had considered Anna quite unmarriageable - a wild spirit that would bite as quickly as it kissed.

The fear began to set into his gut; he felt stricken, nearly ill at the thought of his desire for Nadia leading down that same, disastrous path. He swallowed hard, grasping his head as the thoughts came; tears, tears flowed at his cheeks as he remembered Anna. He looked to Nadia - so peaceful in her sleep, and he knew all at once that nothing good could come of this. He'd never be for Nadia what he hadn't been for Anna - or for any woman. She would find only disappointment in a life at his side.

He laid onto his back, sighing deeply. He had taken something from Nadia she could never again have by making love to her, and now regret stewed in his stomach. She had given him something so precious - and he could never repay her for it. The doubt shrouded his senses like the storm shrouded the moors; the clouds flooded him with loathing instead of rain, chilled him to the bone. He saw beautiful Nadia's face as the last light of the fireplace highlighted her young features, and in that face, he suddenly saw Anna - laughing, laughing at him. Telling him he'd been a fool to think he could ever make a woman happy again.

Gently, Lord Beckham lifted himself from the couch, one step after the other; he found his shirt, thrown onto the floor, still lain in a puddle of pooling rainwater. He wrung the garment out, leaving it creased with wrinkles; nonetheless, he hastily buttoned it onto his body.

It felt cold on his skin, but he needed something - anything, to still the pounding burst of his hot heart. He had decided that all of this had been a great mistake - one he had foolishly led himself straight into. He straightened his breeches and pulled his boots back onto his feet, exhaling sharply. As the fire died away he pulled from the pile another log and threw it upon the stack, watching as those few sparking embers remaining ignited the dried wood in another flash of yellow-orange.

That should be enough to keep her warm until she awoke, he thought.

He wouldn't let her down, the way he had let Anna down. And he knew she could never love him - but he would give her something she could at least appreciate. Something to make up for this twisted system that left her a prisoner; the twisted system that had estranged his dear sister. He'd make it up to Leah, and to Nadia; he'd make it up to everyone, even if he could never be good enough for them.

A marriage of convenience... he thought, it's the only way he could make Nadia truly happy.

"Are you leaving me already?" the sweet voice broke in to his dour thoughts, and he glanced suddenly to the couch, catching sight of Lady Havenshire beneath his coat, smiling. "But we've only just gotten to know each other, Lord Beckham..." she teased. His heart throbbed weakly; he had hoped to be away before she awoke, to deal with this, so that he need not face the pain of hearing her beautiful voice, or seeing her beautiful face, and being reminded of how he would be destined only to fail her.

"I... m'lady, I'm glad you're... awake," he murmured, without conviction. She smiled and crawled off the couch, looking through the window; he admired her, watching her naked rear as she held the coat to her front and strolled towards the window.

"The storm's stopped has it? Quite opportune, I suppose," she smirked. "My father will be wondering what we've been doing..." her impish smirk widened.

"He'd not be quite enamored with me if he knew the truth," Lord Beckham admitted shamefully, his words short and stilted. Lady Havenshire smiled and sashayed in his direction, laying her head against his chest; he felt rigid, nervous, not reciprocating the gesture.

"Nonsense, he's been trying to marry me off to you since the moment old Henrietta began gabbing in his ear," she chuckled.

"We're not married yet, m'lady," he rather sharply pointed out.

"And? I'm a fiery spirit, after all. Father thought me unmarriageable. Perhaps you'll prove him wrong some day?" she said with a silly lilt to her tone, looking up at him with beaming, pretty eyes. It hurt him so greatly to see how much she had begun to adore him, for he knew what he needed to do. For her own good.

"...Perhaps," he said, after a long moment of tense silence. "We... we should return to the estate together, I believe."

"We should," she said with a joyous little giggle, collecting her messy riding clothes. He watched her, so much want in his eyes.

He didn't want to break her heart... but he knew she would be better for it. He didn't deserve her love.

CHAPTER SEVENTEEN

"I've not been to this part of the estate in so long!" Nadia exclaimed as Shadow galloped lazily through the long fields of tall, swaying grasses. "Well... save for the brief few moments of Shadow dashing through it this afternoon," she chuckled. Her eyes bright and her expression full, she felt a contentedness in her heart she hadn't felt... perhaps in her entire life. This, she believed, must be what love feels like; this fullness pressing the inside of your chest, begging to be let out, and she wanted so dearly to simply scale the tallest rolling hill in the Emerys estate and let out a great cry that she had fallen deeply for someone so special, so different than the rest.

Shadow trotted along, whinnying happily as the clouds broke and the sun began to shine, just as night began to fall; a beautiful sunset soaked the sky, beams of brilliant orange and pinks cresting through deep-black clouds. Her heart filled with life and she looked to her lover's face, wanting to see if he was enjoying the sight on the horizon as deeply as she.

Instead, she found an expression she could only charitably described as... very troubled. She had noticed it in the cabin, though she wanted to say nothing; she had noticed it as muddy Pierre pulled himself out of the rain, as they began to trot through the forest. Her life had been turned upside-down, and in a wonderful way, by the man trotting along at her side, but he seemed only distressed at what had happened between them.

"Don't you love rainstorms, Marshall? They seem to be just about as deep and dark and gloomy as you are," she teased in a childish little tone, trotting up alongside him, again showing off just how skilled a rider she was compared to him. While these jokes and his own failure at matters equestrian had brought them smiles of joy and laughter only hours ago, since their moments spent together in the cabin something profound had changed about the man she had come to appreciate so deeply. She expected one of his deadpan, chuckle-worth responses to her little taunt, but she got nothing; he appeared utterly lost in his own thoughts, and when she drew too close for him to ignore her any longer, he startled from whatever dark reverie had cloaked his mind.

"Gloomy? I suppose," he said half-heartedly, giving a forced smile.

"Are you... quite alright, Marshall? Has the rain storm or... some other manner, of happening, put you off of our conversation?" Nadia asked with worry, fearing she had perhaps not been what he had hoped in their intimate moments together, her own insecurities playing deep at the creases of her face.

"I'm quite alright, Lady Havenshire," he responded, dour. Lady Havenshire? She didn't enjoy hearing him call her that, no. She wanted to hear Nadia, the same way he had crooned it as they lay together, cloaked in need for one another.

"Are you worried my father will be cross with you, Marshall?" she whispered to him. He trotted along on lazy old Pierre, sighing and shaking his head.

"I've no worries about your father, no. He seemed quite agreeable to any... arrangements, being made between us," he spoke obliquely. Arrangements? What manner of trouble had befallen the duke to speak in such a manner?

"What manner of arrangements did you have in mind?" Lady Havenshire prodded at him as Shadow paced ahead.

"...We'll discuss it another time perhaps, m'lady," Marshall insisted. Silence fell; it remained with them as they paced back across the moors, through the grasslands, making the trip back to the stables. The entire trip, made in silence, and the doubts began to return to Nadia's mind. She had been so sure, in those loving and lusting moments together in the cabin, that she had finally found something special, but she began to fear for herself. She remembered Ms. Mulwray's urgings in her youth - men are animals, who will take from you what they wish, and you'll never know that they've selfishly availed themselves to you until it's too late.

Nadia thought and thought on it, with only the occasional horse-clops and whinnies to accompany her worried introspection.

When they arrived at the stable they remained silent; she had begun to wonder if these same doubts had been what had driven Lord Beckham to silence. Monsieur Therriault emerged from the stables with a yawn, welcoming the pair back with a tired grin.

"You must've 'ad quite a long day, what with the storm!" he proclaimed with a devious grin. Lady Havenshire gave him a sideways glance and a nervous smile; Lord Beckham simply dismounted poor Pierre, who laid immediately in the dirt, much to Monsieur Therriault's chagrin. "Lazy creature!" he exclaimed.

"We found an old cabin out in the wood and took refuge and... talked," Lady Havenshire commented, her words empty and distant.

"Ah, talked, eh?" the horse-keeper said. Lady Havenshire looked back and noticed that the duke had already left and begun to scale the path back to the manor; she hurried along behind him without another word, only hearing Monsieur Therriault berating Pierre with a string of French expletives.

"M'lord! I... I had wondered, how you intended to handle the conversation, with my father," Lady Havenshire said breathlessly, "about quite... what we had been doing, during the rainstorm? I had not thought on it, until the stable-keeper just asked," Lady Havenshire tried to pry more jokes, or conversation, or anything at all from Lord Beckham, who strode unfettered towards the manor.

"Your answer seemed to convince Monsieur Therriault just fine," he answered nonplussed, before returning to silence.

"Are you certain everything is fine? You don't seem to be fine," Lady Havenshire insisted, her worry beginning to transform into ire. What business had he to treat her so cross after the afternoon they'd had together? She began to fear she had failed him in some way, as they crossed through the garden, the doors to the manor opening wide. Lord Havenshire sat on the couch, as if he had spent the whole afternoon waiting anxious for the pair to return.

"Ah! Lord Beckham, Nadia, it's a pleasure to have you back," he announced, in a manner transparent enough that she could tell it had been rehearsed. Defeated and tired, Nadia began to feel like an actress, dragged through a disastrous production by some manner of trickery. With a bit of confused venom, she glanced at Lord Beckham, who stood still in the doorway, watching her father; never looking into her eyes.

"Father, is Mary about?" Lady Havenshire asked.

"Here, m'lady," came a loud pronouncement from a young maidservant with bushy blonde hair, emerging from the shadows of rear of the foyer. "Have you need of something, miss?"

"Will you see me back to my bedchamber, please? I'm quite ready to retire after the day I've had," she announced loudly, looking back expectantly at Lord Beckham. She hoped to see something - anything, expressed in his eyes. Instead, he simply stood silent; unmoved. She sighed.

"Certainly, m'lady," Mary exclaimed, bumbling nervously towards the stairs. Lady Havenshire follows, each of her footsteps echoing, daggered, through the hallway. She looked back once more - longingly, wantingly - and caught sight of Lord Beckham again, hoping to see anything. Please, she thought; please, just say something. Just say anything, Marshall. I thought I loved you... I want to love you.

He said nothing.

With a flourish and a humph Lady Havenshire stormed down the hall, Mary rushing along behind her. The young maidservant had a thousand questions, no doubt begging for tidbits of gossip to share with the rest of the house staff once Ms. Mulwray retired for the evening.

"M-m'lady! W-was that the man who--" Mary hurried along behind Nadia, nearly out of breath with how quickly Nadia fled the foyer. "The man who's interested in courting you? Lord Beckham?"

"You know his name, do you? Quite good ears the girls down in the maidservants' chambers have, don't they?" Nadia bit back quickly.

"He's-- he's so handsome! I've never seen a noble with a face, or features, like that, not any around here, at least," Mary commented. "Do you think he's handsome, m'lady? I think he'd be quite the envy of any girl down in the servant quarters."

"Yes, he's far nicer to look upon than the normal sort of buckteeth, cheap suit-wearing, wormish men one tends to find among the manors and dinner banquets around these parts," Nadia sighed. The serving girl giggled, certainly loving the titillation of learning something so scandalous about the madam of the house.

"Your father, when I was a little girl, he was the most handsome noble I had ever seen, but I think Lord Beckham is even more handsome," Mary chattered. They rounded a corner and Lady Havenshire pulled open the door to her bedchamber with a grunt, flowing into the room angrily, landing in a fluid, quick motion onto her bed, staring at the ceiling with a disaffected sigh. Mary entered after her, quickly pulling the door shut, hoping excitedly for a gossip session with Lady Havenshire. Instead, Nadia quickly and quite bluntly asked her own question.

"Mary, pardon the particularly personal query, but," Nadia said rather nonchalantly, "have you ever been intimate with a man before?" Mary giggled loudly, her cheeks blossoming in a bright burst of cherry-red embarrassment.

"M-m'lady! I'm..." she gasped, covering her lips. "I'm not... certain, if I am meant to answer that question, or if it's s... simply..."

"You can speak freely, Mary, in fact I prefer that you would be honest, and of course I'd never hold your answer against you," Lady Havenshire assured her.

"Y... yes, m'lady, I've been intimate with men, before," she replied, her voice full of shame.

"You've nothing to be ashamed of, Mary. You're a grown woman, and you're free to find men handsome and interesting, I certainly wouldn't hold it against you," Nadia said. "I have a... query," she continued hesitantly, "about... the first man you were intimate with. How often did you interact with him after?"

"The first man? Oh, he had been a friend of mine for some time," Mary recalled; the line of questioning clearly unsettled the maidservant, whose voice grew unsteady as she began to pick up odds and ends left scattered about Lady Havenshire's bedroom, pulling linens from the corner and idly ensuring the surfaces to be dust-free. "We've... not spoken, often, since then," she said; the manner of her speech suggested to Nadia Mary had not thought much on the subject until prompted. "...I don't see him as much as I used to."

"Do you think there's a reason for that, Mary?" Nadia pressed her, glancing up from the bed.

"I'm... not well-versed in the manner of men," Mary laughed nervously. "I suppose... some men, are simply... well, they've an idea of what they wish to have, and once they've gotten it, they move on with their lives. Perhaps that's what... my friend, thought. The other serving girls, they've... mentioned it, of how men have treated them. It's an unfortunate part of how the world is, I wager." Mary pondered, before blushing embarrassingly. "Men of the sort I spend time with, anyway. I'm certain the kind of gentleman you'd find would be quite different, m'lady. Why do you ask?"

"No reason in particular," Nadia said dismissively, though the reason proffered weighed quite heavily in her mind. She felt embarrassed herself, having such little experience in these matters; she had spent her years abroad studying, thinking, learning about the wild ideas the world had to offer, but when it came to matters of the sexes and of relationships, she found her own viewpoint quite lacking. She hadn't even considered so crass a thought before the sight of Lord Beckham had enticed her so deeply.

Had she been used?...

CHAPTER EIGHTEEN

"You'll never be the man you think you are, or the man you ought to be!"

Those words, fallen from the mouth of his love Anna, stuck with him; they hurt him, crippled him. He imagined that day with her; he had found her rather inebriated and in a compromising position with Lord Rossing, a man he had only ever held the foulest of contempt for. He had retrieved his love, but her actions had brought great sorrow to his heart. He asked her if she had ever truly loved him.

She said she had.

"Anna, please," he pleaded; scaling the stairs of Berrewithe Manor he followed her to her room, only to find she had locked the door shut. "I'll... I'm sorry," he pleaded, pressing his shoulder against the door, longing to feel her body against his once more. "I love you... I want to have your hand in marriage, Anna, doesn't that mean anything to you?"

"Of course it does! I find that you think otherwise to be quite insulting," her voice, muffled, rumbled through the locked door.

"M'lady, I didn't-- I would never intend to insult you, please," Lord Beckham pleaded.

"If you hadn't meant to insult me you wouldn't have questioned my integrity over matters so simply as an evening with Lord Rossing!" she sniped back, her voice hysterical.

"Anna, please... I'm... sorry, I..." his heart throbbing, he couldn't bring himself to break his last barrier; to let her take so complete a control over him. He had to stand up for himself, he thought... he couldn't simply let another man have his wife so thoughtlessly. But he couldn't bring himself to do it; to chastise her. He loved her too deeply, and so caught was he in her spell that nothing could break it.

"You can't even apologize properly for something so outrageous!" she shouted.

"I..." he withered against the door, falling to his knees, eyes full of tears. Ms. Cauthfield had warned him of the woman and her capricious cruelty; of her manipulations. Still, he couldn't say no to someone he loved so deeply.

"Won't you ever say you're sorry for wronging me?" Anna shrieked through the door.

"You're not going to apologize, are you?" Ms. Cauthfield emerged from the shadows, having listened to the conversation. "She's devastated you, m'lord! Spending the evening with another man? She's using you," Ms. Cauthfield whispered. Broken, Lord Beckham looked up to his loyal servant; a woman who had helped raised him, a second mother.

"What am I to do, Ms. Cauthfield? I love her dearly. She is everything to me," Lord Beckham pleaded, tears at his eyes.

"You deserve loyalty, m'lord. Anyone - man, woman, or otherwise - who gives love, deserves love back," Ms. Cauthfield excoriated him.

"Marshall? Marshall! How dare you ignore me!" Anna screamed through the door. Lord Beckham's expression fell, his voice cowed.

"I'm... sorry."

His eyes flashed open, that fetid reverie still clinging like spores of mold to the back of his mind. She had been right, all along; she had broken him, and he knew he could never make a woman like Nadia happy. Anna had been his nadir, but she had taught him that his love would never be enough.

Worse yet, he had claimed the woman's first time; something which had grown to a great storm of dread in the depths of his churning stomach. Since returning to the manor he had drowned himself in loathing for being so crass, so short-sighted, as to steal one of the most sacred things to a young woman! The more the panic set into him the more he convinced himself of the need to settle this the only way he could now, without ruining Nadia's life as he had ruined his own, and his sister's.

"She's quite a creature, isn't she? Takes after her mother, who had all those same, wild, unmarriageable characteristics," Lord Havenshire's hoarse laugh echoed through the hall as night began to creep across the moors. Watching night fall at the top of the stairs, where a towering window gave him view of night's silvery lunar eye, Lord Beckham turned at the sound of the old man's voice, his dark coat bathed in the moonlight.

"M'lord," he said with a nod.

"Quite a storm we had today, hmm?" the old man nodded knowingly, excitement crisscrossing his worn, pale face as he hobbled weakly up the stairs to try to join the younger man. "Did you and my daughter manage to find refuge from the rain somewhere safe?"

"Thankfully so, though unfortunately not before taking a bit of the storm on my back, as you might be able to tell," Lord Beckham chuckled humbly, glancing down at his own rather frumpy-looking, still-damp shirt. "Your daughter is... quite the rider."

"She bloody ought to be, given all the money and time she spent on lessons!" Lord Havenshire commented with a laugh. "I can only imagine how the two of you managed to pass the time."

"We found a gameskeeper's cabin out in the wood," Lord Beckham responded hesitantly. "It had... a fireplace, and some firewood still, thankfully. We talked. It's... been a pleasure getting to know her, and for your sake I feel we may wish to speak in your study, if you have one available." Lord Havenshire's face lit up.

"I think you'd make Nadia the happiest woman in all northern England. Ms. Mulwray, she might have a tendency towards the shrewish at times, but she's got quite an eye, and she regaled me today with a story of just how excited Nadia was to see you this morning," the elder lord exclaimed. The more he spoke, the more uncomfortable Lord Beckham grew. "Have you a mind for pursuing her, then? Let's away to the study for some brandy," Lord Havenshire offered, struggling to drag himself along the stairs.

"It's not quite..." Lord Beckham's words caught in his throat; he didn't quite know how to explain the situation to the sickly old man. Your daughter is wonderful. She's far, far too wonderful for me. But I know of your predicament. I don't want to disappoint her, or you; I don't want to shame her. At least I can help make her happy by giving her freedom. He wished he could say it aloud; instead, he only thought on it as the ailing duke led the two of them through the corridors in a weak hobble. He seemed more ill each time the two of them met, and that only exacerbated the worry in his heart. Need to do this quickly.

"Here we are, the coziest room in all the manor," Lord Havenshire exclaimed in his rasp, hurrying to set upon one of the two armchairs facing a roaring fire, bookshelves and desks arrayed along the walls. Lord Beckham quickly took to one of the writing desks, searching for pen and inkwell, drawing a piece of parchment along the desk.

"I've a proposal for you, and for your daughter, m'lord," Lord Beckham said, as the old man nearly collapsed into the chair behind him.

"Come, there's no need for a rush! I'll have Ms. Mulwray get one of the serving girls to grab a pair of glasses for us and a bottle of some of the finest the cellars have in stock. This is a time for celebrating, after all!" Lord Havenshire exclaimed. Lord Beckham realized that the old man had come to hope his daughter would fall in love... that the marriage would be fruitful for the two of them. Perhaps she had... but he knew no matter how much love the two of them held, love could never work for him. Anna had made sure to show him that this - a marriage just for the sake of name and title - is the most he could do for a woman. At least he could make himself useful in some manner.

"M'lord, it's fine, I don't think this will take long," Lord Beckham insisted, scribbling out the terms as quickly as he could. He took to phrasing them as succinctly as necessary, putting to paper the thoughts he had in his head, but couldn't dare speak aloud.

"I must confide, Lord Beckham, I had little doubt you'd find her manner agreeable - or, at least agreeable as any manner of lord in this entire nation would find her agreeable," Lord Havenshire coughed out with a laugh. "Below the skin, and the fire, and all those wild ideals she carries in her head, she's one of the gentlest, sweetest, and most dedicated hearts you'll find. She came all the way back, here, to England," he continued, "...simply on hearing her father wanted to see her. Of course, I had much... more dire need of her, than I had let on in my letters," Lord Havenshire admitted, as Marshall scribbled hastily across the piece of parchment. The ailing lord's words stung, each of them a reminder of his own failings; that he would fail so beautiful and wonderful a woman as Nadia. "I'm fortunate to know a man like you will be taking care of my Nadia, and the estate, once things... well, once I'm gone."

"There's no need to be fatalistic, m'lord. Nadia will have what she wishes," Lord Beckham insisted, finishing the last lines. He drew an 'x' and a line at the bottom of the contract, drawing a line across it and scribbling his name to the terms he had drawn up - then left another empty line for Lord Havenshire, and another for Nadia. He turned abruptly and offered the page to Lord Havenshire, who began to read its terms with a face full of mirth.

"May it be known Lord Marshal Beckham, Duke of Berrewithe, and Lady Nadia Havenshire of Emerys, be joined into a contract of matrimony to be consummated at the nearest church - oh, consummated, I like that," Lord Havenshire smiled, "and maybe it be known that their marriage be one of... financial, marital convenience, for the method of keeping title, and that Lady Nadia Havenshire shall be known as steward of Emerys, bound not by the usual... sorts of marital expectations..." Lord Havenshire's voice fell away as he continued to read the terms; Lord Beckham recalled them in his head, and when the old man finished, he nodded.

"A marriage simply for your daughter's convenience. For your title, wealth, and lands. She'll not be beholden to me. She'll be free to court and to live as she pleases. I'll have... well, nothing to do with her. It's... best this way, m'lord," Lord Beckham painfully insisted; he felt warmth in his cheeks as a melancholy struck him, as if tears threatened to well over his eyes and splash upon the pages of the contract. "I only want to make her happy."

"B... but, m'lord, Beckham, certainly you don't think my daughter would be happy with this? Ms. Mulwray..."

"I feel she was mistaken about your daughter's... excitement, perhaps. I don't... think, I'm the man that your daughter would want - far from it, m'lord. But for your sake, and for hers... I want to ensure everything is good and proper before anything dreadful should happen to you," Lord Beckham pleaded; he kept his voice stern and settled, though he felt a fire raging inside of him. He realized all too deep in his gut that he had fallen for her; that he had begun to love this wild firebrand, and that he shared her father's disillusionment.

But he knew this is how it had to be, in this twisted world they lived in.

"Lord Beckham, did you... not get along, with my daughter, today? Did... something happen?" the shocked old man asked through a cough. "I was certain you would... grow to... love her," he said, his words limp and pained.

"We... we got along fine, m'lord. Knowing your daughter... this is what she wants. It's what's best for her," Lord Beckham said resoundingly. He could see the heart break in the father's eyes as he came to terms with the contract. "If you'll sign it, and have Nadia do the same, we can have a wedding publicly, if you like... or privately. Whichever is simplest for her."

"I just don't... understand, I suppose," Lord Havenshire sighed. "My daughter... she deserves love. I had hoped I would see it, before I died. Her face... experiencing that amazing feeling. Do you know it, Marshall?" Lord Havenshire asked, crestfallen. Lord Beckham looked away, stilling his raging heart.

"I should really be off for the eve, m'lord," he evaded answering the question deftly.

"You won't stay the night? Certainly, it's too late to be out among the moors. Bandits often prowl these roadways at night, and the sheriff..."

"I should be off," Lord Beckham insisted.

"...Very well," Lord Havenshire said with a weak sigh, a coughing fit claiming him.

"It's been a pleasure, m'lord," Lord Beckham said.

"... A pleasure," the ailing man replied.

CHAPTER NINETEEN

The day broke and the sun draped across Lady Havenshire's body, still lain atop the sheets as she had been while speaking with Mary. She'd drifted away; the day had been exhausting, even life-changing; but worry knotted her stomach the moment she rose from the bed, worry over the nature of her relationship with the man who had claimed her intimately for the first time; the man she found herself helplessly falling in love with.

Men can be animals... men can take what they want and leave. Ms. Mulwray had said the same thing; had warned the girl against being taken advantage of. Nadia considered herself far too strong, far too independent to ever be taken advantage of by something so simple as a man, or silly concepts like love.

Of course, it's those too full of hubris and confidence who often fail to see those signs. Her self-doubt welled up as a sickness in her stomach; she longed to see him, and hoped that, perhaps, he had stayed the eve in the guest-rooms on the grounds. That would give the both of them an excellent chance at speaking about the issues that had come up between them; perhaps they could clear the air, and reignite whatever passion had wavered after their intimate time together in the cabin. A knocking on the door alerted her and she sprung from the bed, still clad in her messy riding uniform; she pulled it off, throwing it into a pile in the corner, grasping at her collection of soft, silken-white gowns to face the day with.

"Who is it?" she asked, her heart ringing hopeful that she'd hear a man's deep, stormy voice on the other side of the door.

"M'lady, your father wishes to see you," came the prickly and stern response. Ms. Mulwray's voice proved not nearly as pleasant as Lord Beckham's, and the harsh tone of her gave pause to young Nadia, who held in her churning stomach a strange little bit of excitement for today's events, hoping to reaffirm her love for the man who had showed her what it meant to be close; showed her just what love could feel like.

"I'll be down in just... a moment, Ms. Mulwray," she responded, her voice shaky. The tone had upset her, and she hastily threw on whatever garment she could get ahold of, running her hands down to smooth the rumples and curls; glancing in a mirror, she paid particular attention to herself; her hair still a mess, her skin dirty, her face tired... she could never present herself to Lord Beckham like this, she thought. Her nerves alight and her heart thumping, she yet hoped she could see him - perhaps he would accept her, no matter how desperate she looked. Her dreams had not been kind; that simmering fear in her stomach had turned to wild dreams of abandonment; Mary's words had made her imagine the duke leaving, never to speak to her or the house staff again.

She contemplated the dream as she fixed her hair, wrapping it into a small bundle with a pretty yellow ribbon. He wouldn't do that, would he? Certainly not. He couldn't! Not when he'd so intimately spent time with her; not when her father had searched him out so. He couldn't do that.

Or perhaps that was the simple girl inside of her talking; the girl with no knowledge, no understanding of relationships. The words of a hopeful heart crying out for him, while her stomach turned, unsure of what to expect when she left her bedchamber.

"He's waiting in the study, and he's quite fragile this morning, m'lady," Ms. Mulwray warned, her eyes focused deeply on Nadia. "Don't set him to desperation today, please."

"Father, yes... is Lord Beckham in the manor? Or in Emerys, perhaps? Did he stay the evening?" Nadia asked tensely, searching the hallway for any sign of the nobleman. Ms. Mulwray's expression flooded with confusion.

"Did you expect him to?" Her words struck Nadia like a resounding cudgel thudding against her head; he hadn't stayed... of course he hadn't. What a stupid girl I'd been, Nadia thought, to expect him to. She walked along the corridor like a tormented revenant; slow, plodding steps, searching endlessly for a love she began to fear she had lost. Why wouldn't he stay? Had he not wished to see her? Wouldn't a man in love be dying to sleep so near to his lover? Wouldn't a man in love spend his waking moments begging, pleading to see his love once more?

She arrived finally at the door of her father's study; she could hear the crackle of its fireplace. The sound triggered memories; her pulse pounded harder, and she imagined his body, strong and nude, so close to hers; his tongue pleasing her as she begged for him never to stop, as they shared quiet words of love and devotion and emotion, words she had never dared say to any man for fear of what he might try to take from her. She hadn't felt that with Marshall; she had found in him a spirit she thought would reject her or use her.

Dread filled her stomach at the thought that he had just been another man... that her worst fears had been true, that all men had the same wicked thoughts and feelings in their head. She took a deep breath and pushed her way into her father's study. He sat in the armchair, swirling a glass in his hand; a piece of parchment grasped in the other, lost in thought. He didn't even notice her at first, something that... rather startled her, and so she began to speak to catch his attention.

"I heard Lord Beckham left last evening? Has he sent word of a safe arrival? The bandits in the moors tend to be ruthless in the evenings," she asked, her words shaky, as she tried so hard to maintain the confidence her father knew her for.

"He's made it back, I'm certain," Lord Havenshire murmured absentmindedly.

"Are you certain? The bandits..." her voice trailed.

"Nadia, I wanted to... to congratulate you - you've found a husband," her ailing father said. "It's a day for celebration. You should be proud."

"Wh... what?" Nadia blinked. "A husband?" She stormed towards her father, her expression stern. "What manner of trickery is this, father?"

"Trickery? There's... no trickery. I've thought on it all evening, and I've signed the contract. Lord Beckham authored this, and he... he told me, it's what you wanted. What would be best for the both of you," he said. He handed the document gripped in his fingers to her, and she snatched at it with a slow, nervous rage building in her chest, the pressure pushing out the love and replacing it with terror. Her eyes pored over the words and with each sentence she felt the urge to scream; she felt pain filter into her, and she nearly collapsed as she finished reading.

Marriage of convenience. Marital freedom. No obligations._She felt... used. As if he'd relieved his guilt over his sister - his guilt over his manhood in a system that favored him - by writing out a silly contract and dismissing her. She had given him something so important, something she had never given any man - something she didn't *want*_to give to any other man, but him. Not just her body, not just the most sacred of covenants; but her love, something she'd never felt.

Now whatever scars he bore had ruined all that and it made her feel... broken. She had felt rage, she had felt bitterness; but now, all she wanted was simply to shrivel away as a flower blustered by a harsh winter.

"I only... wanted to see your face happy, some day, Nadia. I had hoped it could be with him... he seemed to understand you, like no other suitor," Lord Havenshire lamented sadly.

"Father, I... I don't know, why he would do this, our day... together, we..." she huffed, exhaling sharply. "I don't understand this. It doesn't make sense! Why would he want?" She held her fists tight, shaking. "I... I can't... Egan!" she shouted through the doorway.

"Nadia, please, as much as it pains me, at least let me have the opportunity of giving you a wedding," Lord Havenshire pleaded.

"I'm preparing a carriage," she said in a flurry," destined for his manor. We're going to discuss this. I'm... I'm sure it's simply a misunderstanding," she murmured. "...Certainly."

But had it been? As she stormed through the halls, barking for Egan to prepare a carriage, she thought on darker things. Had Mary been right? If the man who had her had claimed her virginity and simply left her afterwards, not to speak to her again...

How could you be so stupid? Lady Havenshire asked herself, swallowing hard. She had been sweet-talked right into the place that he had wanted her. He had gotten what he wanted - and now he had left.

No. He couldn't have. She would get to the bottom of this.

CHAPTER TWENTY

"Has something happened between you and Lord Beckham, m'lady?" Egan asked, breaking his little, jaunty whistle of his favorite tune. It was a bad time to ask such a question of Lady Havenshire, who had spent hours now as a nervous disaster; she had boarded the carriage with breath heavy and heart throbbing, full of fear and full of rage about the pithy contract that the man she had fallen in love with left behind to be signed. A marriage of convenience. Loveless. Hardly a marriage at all. She found it odd, the more she thought on it, that she had ever thought of such an arrangement as attractive at all! Who would enter into bonds so deeply-held, without love to bind it together? She couldn't believe that he would do such a thing! Hadn't he fallen in love with her, just the same as she had fallen for him? Hadn't he felt that spark, like the flash of flint and tinder against the dried wood, erupt into a heart-gripping fire, just as she had? Hadn't he said those adoring words to her by the light of the raging flames, as thunder cracked and rumbled in the distance, rattling the windows to the cabin?

He'd promised her everything. He'd called her a goddess, and he worshiped her just the same. And now he proposed a loveless marriage, simply for the inheritance of name and title? Her heart hurt, and she fought away tears, spurred on by Egan's poorly-timed question. He glanced back as the carriage pulled through the mountains and rocky pathways leading up the hills towards the Berrewithe estate; seeing redness staining her eyes and flowing along her cheeks, he took sudden alarm.

"M'lady, has something happened? Should we turn around?" he queried, full of worry.

"No! No," she shouted insistent, her voice wracked and ragged from the warbling of her angry, melancholy voice. "We've got to see Lord Beckham. He needs to speak with me, to answer for... for this," she said, voice harsh and shrill, waving the contract - she'd taken it with her, if only to throw it into his face as she cried at the loss of love.

"M'lady-- he's asked for your hand in marriage, hasn't he?" Egan questioned curiously.

"It's not that simple, Egan. To him, I'm just a convenient excuse for his guilty conscience, for taking advantage of his sister - and this... this contract, it's just him relieving himself of guilt for taking advantage of me," she shouted.

"M'lady, I'm... isn't that what you... wanted? To have a man in marriage, but not to stifle your life?" Egan questioned. She swallowed hard; her throat hurt from the shouting, and the tears, but she had to say it; if only to hear herself say the words aloud.

"I... I don't want that, Egan. I love him," she said, quivering. Surprise in the portly porter's face, he turned to the horses, coaxing them along the roadway faster.

"We'll get you to the manor, m'lady," Egan called back to her, the horses picking up pace until they practically bounded forward, along the hills and rocky roadways, the carriage bouncing wildly along the path. The vehicle came to an abrupt stop as Egan called out to the creatures who whinnied loudly, the creaking wheels spinning their last as the hasty chauffeur unlatched the carriage door.

"Tell him that, m'lady," Egan pleaded. "Tell him. Any lord who

would turn down true love - he doesn't deserve you, Nadia. Tell him."
She nodded to Egan, who bowed; the doors swung open, and Ms.
Cauthfield emerged from the manor; when she saw Nadia, a wanting
sympathy filled the old woman's face as she dashed across the yard.

"Lady Havenshire, Lord Beckham has..." Ms. Cauthfield sniffled.
"He... he thought you would come to see him, but he's requested... no
visitors, at this time. He's had a difficult time--"

"HE'S had a difficult time?" Nadia exclaimed, the tears still
staining her eyes red. Ms. Cauthfield, face full of regret, full of worry for
her master, shook her head.

"Has he not told you about Anna? About his wedding, in the
Delshire Moors? About..." Ms. Cauthfield appeared broken, fearful. "I
told him... he needed to get past it. I told him, but he never did. And
now he hates himself, and won't have a word with you, Nadia."

"Ms. Cauthfield, I love him," Nadia urged. "I... I truly do love him."
Ms. Cauthfield's face lit up when she heard Nadia's exclamation; she
smiled, even as tears began to stream from the old woman's face.

"He shall have my head for this, but... I'm not going to stop you
from speaking with him," Ms. Cauthfield said, sniffling. "Go, please...
talk to him. Try to break him from this spell that's driven him to
despair... please," she muttered. Nadia pressed past the old woman and
to the front door, pull it open with a flourish, a sudden spark of hope
glimmering in her eye. They could talk; he would be reasonable,
wouldn't he? After all, she loved him.

"Nadia, I should have expected you'd come, and that... Ms.
Cauthfield, bless her, would think it best if I saw you, in spite of my
wishes," Lord Beckham announced, standing at the stairwell of his grand

foyer. He sighed, his voice not that booming, enthralling baritone she had so enjoyed in their first meetings. No, now it felt like a simple shell, a show of false-authoritativeness put on to convince listeners of his sincerity. "M'lady, I don't think... we have much to speak about. Has your father given you the contract? I do believe he... signed it, after I left," Lord Beckham asked. A sea of maidservants and house staff stood at the base of the steps, pretending to work; in truth, few of them could pay attention to their duties, as their attention slipped away to the exchange between the nobles instead.

"Lord Beckham, I don't understand-- we need to speak about this... contract," she said, the words slithering with venom.

"What's not to understand?" he said, brooding, watching farmers and ranchers and workers out on the moors beyond through his window. "I thought this was... well, precisely what you and your father have been looking for. Your freedom... the freedom you deserve as a grown woman. A freedom from the cage you were unfortunately born in to. Your father agreed. It'd be for the best."

"My father agreed? My father agreed because he's an ailing old man! He wants me to be happy, and this isn't happiness!" Nadia shouted.

"It's precisely everything you wanted - and you won't have to deal with me at all. No men to control you - not even I can do that, with the terms I've written here. And I don't want to cage you. I don't expect that of you, or any woman. I'm not worth that," Lord Beckham scoffed dismissively.

"You're not worth... I love you!" Nadia exclaimed angrily. A quiet murmur sounded from the maidservants, who all watched with rapt eyes. "Have you in your stubborn, stupid mind forgotten the things we said together? The feelings that we felt? Was it a lie?"

"I..." Lord Beckham hesitated; he saw the pain he'd wrought, and began to reconsider... if only for a second. His expression vexed, brow furrowed, he turned away. "I can't do that."

"All I am is a convenient excuse for you, then? A way to ease your guilty conscience?" Nadia asked accusingly. "Is that what matters to you, more than my love? To ease the painful memory of your sister, estranged from you over this sordid mess of an estate? To ease the pain, you feel about your past?"

"You are not an excuse," Lord Beckham began to grow angrily resenting at the accusations. "I've done this for you. For your own good. For everything you want. I'm not what you think I am; I'm not what you want," he roared.

"You've spent so much time convincing yourself of that that even love can't break this disgusting self-loathing!" Nadia shouted, storming up the stairs towards him. "I'll not let it happen. This contract - here! I'll not be a party to your self-destruction, Marshall," her voice raised higher and hotter, and with all eyes on her she threw it at his feet. "You lied to me. You used me!"

"I did not use you!" he retorted, turning to face her, his expression torn, shredded by hatred. She could see pain beneath, tears forming at the corners of his eyes.

"You took my virginity! Is that all I was meant to do for you?" The revelation sent a wave of shocked gasps through the assembled crowd of maidservants, their eyes wide. "Is that what you had searched for? And now that you've gotten it, you're quite content, aren't you? That's all you needed," she sneered.

"That had nothing to do with... with any of this, though I... I regret taking you, in that manner," he admitted painfully. "It was a mistake. It shouldn't have happened, and I shouldn't have let it happen. I'll never be good enough for--"

"For what? For me? I said I love you! Am I not the person to make the determination of who is good enough, and who is not?!" Nadia shouted, stamping her shoe's heel into the contract. "I can choose whomever I wish to be good enough for me! Or perhaps you're just like the other men, thinking yourself above a woman? Thinking yourself better equipped to make her decisions for her?"

"And with every word you speak you only prove to me that I made the right decision with that contract - that I've failed you, just as I failed before, and just as I will always fail," he rumbled.

"Why have you set yourself so stringently on this path, Marshall? Why?" Nadia pleaded, tears flowing freely along her cheeks now. "You feel it inevitable that you will fail. Any trouble that befalls you is evidence of that failure; any good fortune is simply luck, or happenstance. You've dedicated yourself so completely to this lie that you'd break my heart for it," she sobbed.

"It's not my choice, Nadia. It's my destiny to fail the ones I love, and I can't put you through that," he lamented. "Please. Let me at least do some good, for you. Some small amount of good. Let me save your father's heart; let me give to you what he wants for you."

"My father wanted me to be happy. Did he not tell you that? The estate -- all of it. He cared more for my heart, for love - than he did for title or peerage," Nadia exclaimed. Lord Beckham struggled, his hands shaking; tortuously close to that precipice or seeing reality, of seeing the heart breaking in Nadia's chest.

"He's a good man... and he will understand me in making this decision," Lord Beckham said, turning his shoulder to the woman as she cried.

"...That's it, then? Ms. Cauthfield... she had hope of saving you. I suppose I did, too. I had hoped, from that first night, that our hearts could find one another. It was only a glimmer of hope, a whisper of it, but I held on to it. The morning we rode together... I had never felt any sort of joy or excitement for so simple, so dull a task. But with you, I saw something. I saw the sun. And you've stifled it; choked the life from it. I loved you."

"This is how it has to be, Nadia. I'm deeply sorry," Lord Beckham insisted. "Please... go back to your estate. Make your father happy. He's a good man. He would like to spend what time he has left with you, I'm certain. We will resolve matters of title, and then you shan't need to see me in your life ever again. You'll be happy, Nadia. That I promise you."

"No, I won't," she spat bitterly as she stormed down the stairs, giving him one last searing look. "You don't have to fail again, and again... but you will, because you insist upon it," she said, and with that she threw open the doors and left the estate, her heart heavy.

CHAPTER TWENTY-ONE

The door to Lord Beckham's bedchamber flung open, he retreated to the only place he knew he could; the only refuge he had from the memories; from the pain. The only place no one could force him to face reality. From the window, he watched her leave the manor's front door; she stormed towards her family's carriage, and she tried so firmly to appear angry; but as she reached the vehicle he watched what lay beneath. He watched her fall to her knees and begin to weep; he could hear her sobs, even at his window, carrying cries of sorrow soaring over the moors. He looked away, swallowing hard, his expression canted towards the carpet; trying to drown out the pain with something, anything; any thoughts.

But everything in his mind came back to her.

He pulled the curtains shut; the sight had only reaffirmed precisely what he had gotten into his head. He would fail; he would always fail. Just as Anna had fled him, racing up the stairs with tears in her eyes. Good, he thought to himself; she had to learn eventually. Nadia would have found herself hating him; it was the only natural consequence, just as it had been before.

He closed his eyes. He felt his own chest welling with emotion; he, too, wished to weep, looking upon another failure. *You'll never be the sort of man a woman will ever want.* He heard her voice calling to him; from the rafters of his bedchamber, shrieking through his dreams, like a ghost he could never escape; a doom he could never hope to outrun. He closed his eyes, but even then, he saw her; now, he saw Nadia, too, her face crossed with tears, stained a blushing red, another ghoulish failure of his past. He heard her berate him, just as he had heard Anna. You only fail because you insist upon it!

He threw himself upon the chair to his writing desk, fighting back the tears and the rage; his hands balled into fists he grasped at his liquor shelf, squat with a door of glass, pulling it open. He thought it the only way of forgetting the dreams; the dreams of failure, dreams that soon would bear home to a new haunting memory, one of the beautiful woman he had taken to the cabin; the beautiful, free-spirited firebrand of a woman whose innocence he had claimed so shamelessly.

He swallowed hard; through flames of tears and rage swelling his eyes and blotting his sight Lord Beckham grasped a bottle of muddy-brown liquor, stoppered with a simple cork. He slammed it upon his desk and took in a deep breath, trying to still his shaking hands and cool the flow of emotion pouring from within him. He examined the glass; examined his hand. He closed his eyes, and she hadn't left him yet; he saw her nude, wriggling in the warmth of the fire, whispering to him just how much she wanted him.

If only she had known.

Trembling he grasped the bottle. He pulled the stopper from its mouth, overpowering and heady scent striking his nostrils. He lifted the foul decanter to his lips, taking a deep and unsteady breath.

Knock knock knock! A pounding upon the door shook him from his destruction and spite-filled reverie, and he gulped loudly as a brief, gleaming sunbeam of reality poured into his widened, melancholy-stricken eyes.

"I've no time for conversations," he replied in a muddied, weak tone. He waited, the haze drifting painfully through his mind. He heard no further protest, and turned his gaze once more to the bottle, the swill stinging his nostrils. He recoiled, before another loud knocking interrupted him.

Knock knock!

"Begone!" he retorted, beginning to fear his demons had coalesced into a hate-gnashing mob, come to drag him to his rightful spot in hell. He focused his mania on the bottle before him, his shaking hands lifting it to his mouth, but before he could sip, he heard the hinges to his bedchamber door squeaking quietly open. He heard footsteps... no, he wouldn't look away. He had made his decision. He would hear no more protest.

"M'lord," came a quiet voice.

"Ms. Cauthfield, I'm not in need of a dressing-down in any sort of fashion at this particular moment," the duke dismissed her with an obstinate venom.

"No, I think you are," she responded, like the bite of an angry beast whose rage had been simmering for some time. The old woman threw the door shut behind her and she charged heedless at her master, slapping the bottle from his hand, sending it careening to the carpet, shattering, its contents spilling and the foul, ichorous smell permeating the bedchamber. Lord Beckham blinked in utter amazement; his mouth agape and astonishment in his eyes, he watched as Ms. Cauthfield, who had spent so long a time as a reticent observer of his self-destructive tendencies, positively seethed at him. She had never seen her so, and it... well, it quite scared him.

"I've watched you struggle along this path alone for far too long,

165

Marshall, and I'll not tolerate it any longer," she sneered.

"Ms. Cauthfield, this is outrageous," Lord Beckham rumbled in protest. "You--"

"No, you're outrageous! You're utterly outrageous, Marshall, and I'll not stand for seeing it any longer," Ms. Cauthfield exhorted him, tears beginning to stream from her own eyes. "I'll not watch you destroy yourself again. That girl loves you!"

"Anna loved me too," Lord Beckham lamented. "Anna--"

"Enough with Anna! Enough! How could your mind be on something from so long ago with a beautiful young girl who's fallen in love with you, pleading to have you? How?!" Ms. Cauthfield exclaimed, and in a sudden surge of emotion the older woman slapped her master across the face, stunning him. Her eyes widened; she couldn't rightly believe her own actions, her wrinkled cheeks reddened with tearful rage. She cleared her throat, shivering.

"Ms. Cauthfield..." Lord Beckham mumbled halfheartedly.

"I'll not... apologize, for what I've done, and if you'll have me dismissed for it, so be it," Ms. Cauthfield said, shaky. "I'd far prefer to be dismissed, to find myself on the streets of London, than to stay in this manor, and watch it die; watch the family I've served loyally my whole life wile away their lives and fortune, to watch the boy I've known for so long give in to his self-hate, to destroy himself, and destroy so true a love as he has right in front of him," she exclaimed through sniffles. Try as she may to maintain her professional dignity, Ms. Cauthfield couldn't let her emotions simmer. "Decades of braised honey beef and scraped knees; decades of service to your father, your mother; to you, and I promised your parents - promised them - I'd watch after you, until I no longer served the Beckham household. And I suppose I shall consider today to be that day, because I cannot simply watch that poor girl walk away, Marshall, because you despise yourself so deeply! Because of that blasted woman, and that day in the Delshire Moors. She never loved you, Marshall! But Nadia, this poor girl, you showed her something she's never seen before," Ms. Cauthfield seethed.

"Ms. Cauthfield, I don't want to dismiss you," Lord Beckham insisted, his voice weak. "I don't..."

"Then I'll offer instead my resignation, for I can't bear to do this any longer," she said shrilly. In a storm was she off, the bedchamber door slamming behind her; Marshall sat in stunned silence for a long and quiet moment, breath caught in his throat. He smelled the rank burn of the liquor rising from the carpet and swallowed hard.

He gathered himself up, and wandered out of the door to his bedchamber in search of the maidservant, but silence crept across the entirety of the manse. In an emotional haze, he stumbled back to the stairwell; deathly silence fell across the chamber, and he spied on the carpet - stamped and ripped - the contract he had drawn up, his own name next to Lord Havenshire's. At the front door stood loyal James, though in his expression Lord Beckham could read the same disappointment with which Ms. Cauthfield had only recently bludgeoned the duke with.

"James," the duke said, acting as if in a trance, his mind addled with some sense of shocked madness.

"M'lord," the butler responded coldly. He saw her in the window... he saw her down the stairs. Always that smile. When Lord Beckham looked upon the dead fireplace at the rear of the foyer, he saw her again; flashes, pained flashes, like the memories of Anna.

He needed to forget Anna, he told himself. Perhaps Ms. Cauthfield had been right.

"A carriage... a carriage," Lord Beckham blurted. He stepped lightly down the stairs, his mind wandering. He could hear Nadia's words echoing through the vaulted ceilings. He saw her face; heard her fiery exhortations.

"A carriage, m'lord, bound for where?" James asked.

"The Emerys estate, I... I need to have Nadia sign this contract," he rambled. "I need..."

"M'lord... I think you need something different," James murmured.

"...Perhaps... perhaps I..." Lord Beckham exhaled.

"Do you love her, m'lord?" James asked.

"I... think, I do," the duke responded hesitantly.

"You'll only ever know what can happen with love if you try," James pleaded. He could only hear her words; every time he closed his eyes he saw her face.

"I think... I do, love her," he shuddered. "But how could anyone truly love me back?"

"You can't let that woman haunt your life forever," James said.

"...prepare a carriage, James... this contract..." Lord Beckham repeated his idea, a curious mantra of self-protection.

"I'll do as you wish, m'lord, but perhaps you should reconsider your course of action," the butler added, before stepping through the grand front doors.

He closed his eyes. He saw her again.

"Perhaps..." Lord Beckham's voice trailed.

CHAPTER TWENTY-TWO

"I'm certain your father will be fine, m'lady," Egan murmured as the carriage pulled alongside the front of the Emerys manor. Her heart shattered, Lady Havenshire had spent the trip back across the moors with her mind awash in rage, in pain; she felt utter loss, betrayal. She had never felt something so acute in her life; something so stinging in her chest as a round and utter rejection.

"Father is going to die, Egan, and all he wanted was to see my face happy before that happened," she lamented with a sigh. "I loved that man. I didn't know what real love meant, and..."

Her mind flashed back to the first night together. How she had treated him harshly after hearing of his sister. She thought of the laughs; the smile, before a darkness crept across them. She thought of his stormy eyes; how she had seen him, a darkness against the backdrop of Lord Perrywise's gaudy and ostentatious ballroom; she had seen something different in him. Had he truly been different? Or had he used her as any man would - in all that ways that Ms. Mulwray had warned?

As the horses' hooves clopped along the roadway, her family manor looming close, she closed her eyes and saw him again. She saw his dusky expression at the far end of the dining hall; she felt in her mouth the sweet succor of honey-braised meat, a recipe that felt as delectable in her imagination as it had in person. She smelled the steam of fresh food, heard the echo of his darkly-commanding tone rolling through the dining hall. His quips took her heart away to a different place; to a better time, to laughter at his expense as he saw the terrified lord atop the back of a lazy, aging horse.

It brought her back to that day. The rains fell and she thought her very life in danger at the spine-tingling chill of the rain across swaying autumn trees. Hearing his voice call out across the forest, like a rescuing lifeline. She saw the old cabin; the smell of mold, spurts of dust; dried wood. She recalled his scent; his body. An exceptional body; one she wanted to wake up next to, every single morning.

"Your father will be waiting, m'lady..." Egan broke into the reverie; they had arrived at the front door of the manor, the horses clopping their hooves impatiently, wanting for the embrace of the stable. Her eyes opened and that memory drifted away, even as he heard in her mind memories of her name burning passionately from his gaping mouth. She shivered, recalling the rainy cold of that day; a cold she felt now renewed, as a breeze passed through the opened door of the carriage. She stared at the face of the manor - it felt flat; everything felt flat, as if all the color and all the life and vigor of all the world had withered away without the thought of him brimming in her mind. The vibrant, burning fiery-oranges and reds of the trees in autumn, the blanket of fallen leaves and swaying yellows of bushes dying away for the season felt dull compared to the fire he brought to her life.

Soon, she thought, winter would come; a freezing blanket of white would claim the bright colors of autumn, washing away warmth and filling bones that had once felt the sudden, lively surge of love with the icy fingers of contempt; of loneliness. Frozen in the unchanging, gray doldrums of that dark time would be her memories of him, gleaming within the frozen wilds, always beckoning her back to that embrace. But she couldn't have them; she couldn't cling forever to fall, for winter would come and claim everything she had loved. It would claim her father, as it had claimed her mother; it would claim her fortune, and her freedom. She'd be a captive bird shrilly squeaking from a crushing cage.

"M'lady..." once more her gloomy recollections fell victim to the quiet, meek tone of the portly man at the head of the carriage. The horses whinnied and waited; dark-gray clouds gathered at the far edges of the sky, and she could hear faint rumblings of thunder threatening to bring back those memories all over again. Wherever a storm brewed, she saw him - the stormy man she had fallen for, who had slain her dreams.

"Yes, Egan, I... I know," she murmured. As she stepped from the carriage a great wind swept up, throwing dust and rotting brown-gray leaves into her messy hair; she exhaled deep, taking a breath of the air; she couldn't taste it, her senses dulled to their depths by the experiences of the morning. She hesitantly stepped towards the door to the manor. Her eyes closed again, the wind whipping against her, her dress clinging to her body; her hair thrown in tangled masses across her shoulder by the powerful gusts.

I loved him, she thought to herself. She wanted to give herself to him - just as they had promised in those hot, tense, wet throes of flaming passion. When he drew his coat atop their quaking bodies she had everything she had ever dreamed of - a true gentleman, one who respected her; one she loved, a man different from the others.

She entered the manor, immediately greeted by the sight of her father - arms spread, hopeful and caring, at the base of the foyer's grand stairwell.

"Nadia! Dear, how... how did everything go?" he asked, his face crested with pain. Clearly, he had hoped to see the two of them return together, and heartbreak filled his expression at the sight of a lone woman standing in the opened doors.

All he had wanted was to see her happy, before he passed. And she had been happy - happy like she never thought she could be, here in England; here in the moors and forests, where the world had been built against her freedom and happiness. But somehow, she had found it - for those few passing days with him, she had found it.

"Father, remember the story you used to tell? About mother?" Nadia asked, the winds gusting across her back. "About how you met."

"Your mother," he chuckled. "Oh, how I miss her... we met not far from here, remember?"

"Tell me," she insisted, her body shaking.

"Come inside, please, Nadia," her father pleaded through a cough.

"Please, father, tell me," Nadia insisted.

"I tripped in her dress and she called me a scoundrel," her father coughed out a laugh. "She hated me. And yet we met, again and again, at dinner parties, and because our parents insisted upon it," he chortled. "You know the story."

"She hated you, but you never gave up, did you, father?" Nadia asked, her voice shaking.

"Love is... a complicated thing, Nadia. It takes dedication, it takes sacrifice, it takes... well, stubborn, persistence," he advised.

"Stubborn persistence? And what's that you once said of me, father?" she demanded. His vexed expression shifted slowly to a warm smile.

"You're the most stubborn young woman I've ever known, Nadia," he responded gently.

"I have somewhere I need to go - I need to be rather stubborn, father," she said with a smile, "as I've a very... stubborn man. A man I love."

"Egan will get you there I'm certain," he replied.

"No, I must move with great haste. Shadow will take me there far faster," she responded, hurrying towards the stables. Her father beamed with pride as the door slammed behind his daughter. He'd finally gotten to see her so awash with that feeling - love.

CHAPTER TWENTY-THREE

"Hyah!"

Lady Havenshire's voice carried across the moors; she raced atop Shadow's back as the horse bucked and brayed anxiously, leaping along the cobblestone paths, through dusty trails and along pathways coated in dead leaves and dying autumn colors. The pathways connecting Emerys to Berrewithe had never seemed so long, so painstakingly jagged and mazelike, as they did now - when she needed to make every second count. She needed to see his face again - to tell him he loved her, and that as a stubborn woman, as stubborn a woman as ever lived in the moors, she wouldn't simply let him decide alone who was worthy of whom. She raced against time; she raced against her own doubts. She raced against a storm brewing at her back - gray clouds had gathered against her, threatening to stop her forced and hasty march across the roads, the thunder rumbling ominously closer and closer each maddening mile her steed traversed.

"Shadow, here! Hyah!" Nadia's mind worked quickly; she spotted a sideways path that she knew cut across the river bank that separated her estate from the wilds between Berrewithe and Emerys. The long and sloping road saw little traffic from carriages and merchants, on account of its steep and awkward slopes, but atop proud Shadow's back Nadia had no doubt the route would prove faster. Dashing past thorny yellowed bushes and tall, unkempt grasses, Nadia and her proud mount barreled through mud and mush and weeds, the storm growing louder with each passing moment. A crackle of blinding lightning frightened both Nadia and her horse, who whinnied loudly at the blaze of white light, but continued on heedlessly. As trees blurred past, she saw him everywhere - in everything. Her father had been right about her - stubborn. Stubborn enough to put herself at great risk... riding alone, a woman along the moors, as a thunderstorm rumbled forward... and worse, taking a rarely-used path carved along a marshy, rock-riddled highway.

Only then, as the blinding blast of white subsided, did Nadia notice the peculiar horseman at the side of the rarely-traveled path, leading his white-skinned horse to drink at the side of the road. Nadia felt it odd... practically none dared travel this roughly-hewn path. Nadia tried not to worry about the sight, though her heart began to thump in her chest when she saw another horseman clad in black, a scarf drawn across his features, further along the path. Lightning flashed blinding again and Shadow stepped through a morass of muddy puddles, her pace slowing briefly before taking to the bridge up ahead - a rickety bridge of crumbling stones drawn across the river bank, the rushing sounds of a shrunken stream gushing along her ears. The bridge rose tall above the stream, and she dashed across it quickly... but a wary glance back took notice of a gaggle of horses gathered at the shadowy arches beneath the bridge, and a gathered group of men in patchwork clothing, their faces masked, swords and flintlocks slung at their waists, scrambling as they saw her pass.

Her heart stopped and terror froze the blood in her veins as a realization struck her hard as a musket-blast to the back. Bandits, she realized too late. So few took this roadway... particularly in the interest of avoiding entanglements with the sorts of bandits who infested the distant paths. At night, the bandits scattered across every roadway, but now Nadia had crossed daringly into their own domain, and they gave chase. Nadia tightened her profile against the horse, urging Shadow on with loud walloping calls, spurring the creature into a fevered run as she heard horse hooves clopping behind her.

The storm... the bandits, and the threat of losing a man's love. They all loomed over her shoulders, chasing her desperately - threatening to claim her love, her comfort, her future, and now - her life.

"Shadow! Hya!" She glanced over her shoulder as she called to her steed, and the bandits dragged slowly behind her; she took a detour from the rough roadway, her horse deftly leaping across a small stream and hopping up a series of stony cliff-faces. Grinning, she looked back and found several of the foul horsemen confounded by the path, their steeds unwilling to brave those same dangers... but a few were gaining on her, and her heart pounded against her ribs. She felt Shadow's pace slowing; Nadia had pushed the poor horse hard, and now her stamina had begun to wane. Her hands shaking, Nadia gripped the reins tight, leading her tired mount back to the roadway. Shadow gave her all, galloping along; even the horse, it seemed, knew the stakes, feeling sympathetic to her loving master's pained plight. A loud crack rang out, but it wasn't thunder; terror in wide eyes Nadia looked back to see the bandits gaining ground, hooping and shouting, firing their pistols in her direction. She swooped to one side, then the other, leading Shadow skillfully along a lower path down a mountain as her pursuers kept close. Another volley of crackles erupted, loud and high-pitched; her breathing met a wild, fevered pitch, adrenaline pumping fear and flight into her every being. She had made a grave mistake, and as the thunderstorm drowned out the sound of the shouting, screaming bandits chasing after her, trying to intimidate her, she closed her eyes.

She saw him; her love, the only one who could still her heart. She wondered in that moment if she would ever see him again.

Shadow whinnied and Nadia's eyes flashed open as a bullet whizzed past, only a mere inch from striking the steed in the flank. She realized that the bandits had no interest in harming her - they instead wished simply to isolate her, kidnap her, so that they might ransom her, or use her for... rather more nefarious purposes. She swallowed hard, gripping with all the strength her body could to Shadow's reins, but she felt Shadow pacing slower, and slower; the bandits laughed as they began to keep pace, surrounding Nadia on each side.

"Shadow! Here, hya!" she directed her horse along a side path, through some trees; the bandits closed rank behind her, but two clumsy riders moved slowly and found themselves acquainted rather harshly with the ground when their steeds stopped suddenly in the thicket of trees, launching their riders careening into the dirt. Still, six men on horses galloped along behind her ailing mount, and when the trees cleared they rode side-by-side now with Nadia, two of them pulling to each side of her.

"Help! Help me! Please, stop," Nadia exclaimed, tears forming at her cheeks. Laughing the laugh only a creature of seething, slimy scum could laugh, one of the bandits pawed at Nadia's breast, trying to tear her from her mount in the lewdest manner he could. She pulled away, kicking at the man and his horse; Shadow whinnied and rammed sideways into the man, though another bandit rode up behind and took his place. They'd surrounded her now, and her chest hurt; her throat grew hoarse as she screamed for anyone to help.

"Oy! Look 'head!" one of the bandits warned his comrades as the others grasped at Nadia, who tried to pull ahead. She couldn't open her eyes; she couldn't dare look at the fate that had befallen her.

"S'time ta have some fun with you, girly!" one of the filthy bandits crooned, moving in close with a sinister laugh on his tongue. Her heart pounding, she gripped Shadow close, listening to the horse's pained cries over the round of horseshoe gallops and sleazy chuckles.

CRACK!

An explosive sound poured across the fields; at first, she took it to be thunder, but she heard a loud crash and looked to her side. The awful bandit who had been keeping pace at her flank shouted in pain as the force of something threw him from his horse; the other bandits fanned out, exclaiming in fright. Another crack rang out - and she recognized it as a musket shot, the bullet striking another bandit and knocking him clean off his horse.

Hope suddenly gleaming in her heart, she looked ahead and saw a carriage pulled off to the side of the desolate roadway. She led Shadow close to the carriage, but the bandits drew closer; she saw no one at the vehicle, but when the mass of horses and bandits passed close enough a man like a wild, confused blur of color appeared suddenly from behind the vehicle, a using the lengthy butt of his musket to ambush one of the bandits, knocking him off his horse with a powerful swing that cracked against the malicious rider's jaw. Her breaths ragged, her chest sore and her eyes reddened and muddled with tears, she swung around in a wide circle, traipsing back in a wide, arcing circle, back to the carriage. The bandits chased her, and as she drew close to the vehicle she leapt from Shadow's back, rolling along the rode with a pained grunt, taking cover beneath the carriage. She closed her eyes, covered her head, hoping that whoever this phantom savior had been, that he hadn't yet vanished before finishing the job. She heard the bandits do the same; their horses whinnying, hooves pattering, she soon heard their feet and their greedy, grubby and wanting exclamations fill the air. The sound of steel drawn against scabbards startled her as the boot falls and growling voices drew closer. Nadia shook, her eyes clasped shut tight, when she heard the voice grow loud.

"Oy, 'ere she is! Get 'er, and whoever helped--" the grungy voice was suddenly and quite violently silenced by a resounding, skull-cracking THUMP. Nadia winced as she heard the noise ring over the rumble of thunder; then, another, and another, as the scuffle grew wilder and faster. She heard a bandit cry out in pain and finally dared to open her eyes, just to catch a glimpse. She saw a single pair of tidied boots amid a dozen scrounging, dirtied feet, squaring off with skillful, quick movements. Another loud CRACK filled the air, sounding so particularly disgusting in what it meant for the recipient of the attack that Lady Havenshire recoiled beneath the carriage in vicarious pain. She saw a bandit drop, his sword clattering to the cobblestones of the road; horses whinnied as they came around for another pass, and she noticed two other groaning bandits, already taken down, crawling helplessly along the roadway, wracked with pain from their encounter with this mysterious savior.

Nadia covered her head as another series of loud thwacks, jerks and spins followed; her eyes closed, she just begged silently for all of it to be done; she wanted just to see Lord Beckham again. A brush with death had perhaps made her realize more than anything that she just wanted to be near him - even if she didn't prove stubborn enough to convince him of her feelings of how they ought to be together, she would give anything to simply see him again before she died; to see the man she had fallen in love with.

Finally, the sound of the violent scuffle subsided, the crack and smack of blunt rifle-butt against bone and flesh replaced by the long, pained groans of battered, beaten outlaws. Horses kicked up dust and dirt, galloping along without their masters upon their backs. When all the chaos seemed to die, Nadia opened her eyes, her breaths quivering, to see if anyone remained standing after the great battle.

She saw only the decimated remains of the melee - men in patchwork armor and weather-beaten cloaks, scarves covering their faces, bruises and welts freshly beaten into each of them as the struggled for consciousness. She didn't see the fresh pair of boots, and feared the worst. Closing her eyes again, she felt tears along her cheeks, murmuring quietly to herself.

"Please. Please. I just want to see him again. Please. Please. I love him. I'll do anything, please, just let me see him again. You can take me, you can kill me, you can do whatever you will, be I just want to see him again, please," she begged, prayed to some silent power, for anything - just a moment of reprieve, just to see him again.

"See who?" she heard boots clasp as the carriage creaked, and her strange savior appeared. She recognized the voice; it filled her heart, brimming with joy.

"You-- wh--" Nadia, startled and confused, saw his face come into view as he knelt down to help her out from beneath the carriage.

"It's not safe for women to travel these paths, you know," Lord Beckham chided her playfully, taking her hand.

"How..." Nadia asked, utterly dumbfounded. He smirked.

"I may not have spent my time learning to ride, m'lady," he quipped, "but I must've spent that time learning to do something worthwhile... right?" he gripped his musket in his free hand, tugging her out from beneath the carriage with the other.

CHAPTER TWENTY-FOUR

Nadia say at the side of the ride, her gown a mess of dirt and dust, admiring the other skill her love appeared to have spent quite a great deal of time practicing - tying knots. More specifically, incapacitated with rope each of the scoundrels who'd survived the battle, wrists bound tightly together and ankles to follow. Groaning in anguish, three of them lay half-conscious and muttering curses at the dutiful duke as he leashed their comrades; she smiled in quiet awe at him, having shown a side she had never yet seen.

"You'll pay for 'is! The other mates'll be 'ere to finish you and yer little harlot off!" one of the wrapped-up bandits angrily protested; Lord Beckham rolled his eyes, quite confidently and unconcernedly striding back to the carriage, grasping the weapon leaned against it, and bashing the rather angry, odious little man in the cheek with the butt of the gun.

"I'd be delighted to see them - I need the exercise, after all," Lord Beckham quipped, exhaling sharply and tossing the weapon to the ground beside him. "Harlot - what sort of language is that for a proper gentleman?" he scoffed jokingly. He threw a glance to his 'harlot', who grinned brightly, her heart full of warmth - but her mind, and her face, wracked with confusion.

"Marshall, it's certainly... pleasant, to discover so many secret talents, of yours," she quipped, her breath still quavering, body still wracked with excitement and fear and bafflement at this precarious turn of events. "Though, I must admit the talent of yours that most entices me in just this moment is your rather mystical power of precognition," she added lackadaisically. Shadow stood at Nadia's side, whinnying and clopping her hooves on the roadway in agreement; Nadia gently tugged on her loyal steed's reins to calm the beast, her heart racing nearly as fast as Nadia's was.

"And just what are you implying of me, Lady Havenshire?" he asked playfully, a bandit groaning as the dutiful duke tugged the ropes binding the scoundrel up tight.

"Nothing, m'lord, simply that I find it rather fortuitous for you to happen upon my predicament, having been traveling the same road, at the same time as I," Nadia coyly murmured, her cheeks blossoming a slight tone of rose. She thought to continue her sheepish little line of curious questions, when she heard a bristling from the brush behind her and nearly leapt in a panic. Glancing to her rear she saw a suit-wearing man wrestling with a tangle of thorny brush, emerging from the forested fields dotting the side of the roadway. Though she kept her guard up at first, she sighed a hefty breath of relief when she recognized the man as James, Lord Beckham's loyal butler.

"M'lord, m'lord, I heard gunfire! Gunfire, and shouts, and, I know you told me to stay hidden in the brush, but--" James blinked as he came upon the rather righteous carnage strewn about the roadway, his master tying down the criminals one-by-one. "--Oh," he murmured in shock, gulping. "I didn't know your fighting skills had come such a long way, m'lord. You must've been practicing." He at once took notice of Lady Havenshire and jumped out of his skin at the sight, shock on his face, followed swiftly by pleasant surprise. "Oh- oh! Lady Havenshire, what a fortunate set of circumstances that we happened upon you at so critical a time," he said. A loud thunderclap echoed through the sky and the winds began to whip quicker and wilder. "Oh, blast it, just my luck," the butler grumbled. "Blast the weather on these miserable moors. Not a day can pass peaceful without thunder grousing on about it."

"Yes, a critical time, just the sort of question I had meant to ask your master," Lady Havenshire said.

"Well, I had need of traveling a quick route back to the Emerys estate, and James suggested this side path," Lord Beckham murmured innocently, hoisting a groggy criminal onto his feet, dragging the man to the carriage and throwing him unceremoniously inside. "James spied a group of roustabouts harassing a young lady, rather roughly, and when I saw them carrying dangerous weapons, I felt it necessary to act," the duke recalled, a hint of the precocious gleaming in the little smile working its way through his steely expression. "Fortunately, the bandits around these parts have far more courage when it comes to harassing lone women, than they do skills with those sabers and pistols they carry," Marshall scoffed.

"You bloody ambushed us, you coward!" one of the bandits grumpily groaned, before receiving a swift kick to the sides by Marshall, who hoisted him up next and threw him into the cabin of the carriage along with his lowlife brethren.

"Ambushed, coward," he joked. "Not, of course, that I wanted you to think I thought you incapable of saving yourself, of course, m'lady," Lord Beckham added playfully. "I'm certain if you'd had the same advantages I had in position, you'd have dealt with them quite as handily as I did. I simply wanted to offer some assistance."

"Your assistance is appreciated, though you glossed over a rather important bit in your explanation, m'lord," Nadia said, breathing deep.

"Did I?" Lord Beckham crossed the road with concern in his face.

"You mentioned that a matter of some importance drove you to seek a faster path to the Emerys estate... or did I imagine that part?" Lady Havenshire asked, her cheeks burning bright pink.

"You did in fact hear correctly," Lord Beckham said, his voice rattled; he could tackle a dozen bandits, but the matters of their affair still shook him to his core. She smiled. She could certainly appreciate that sort of humility in a man.

"And what purpose, might I ask..." she broached the question calm and coyly. "...would you have, being present at Emerys manor, m'lord?" He approached her cautiously, slipping his hand into his jacket and retrieving a piece of paper - crumpled, crushed, and ripped, with ink stained in swirling circles along its surface. He unfolded the parchment and revealed it to be the contract - the one she had thrown at him, had trod angrily upon. She breathed a sigh of displeasure, looking away.

"You haven't signed this contract, m'lady." Suddenly she felt strong hands upon her; grasping her chin, cupping it close, turning her face back in his direction; she resisted, tears welling up again, shivering as another wind pressed along her back.

She winced as she heard the slow sound of him tearing the contract in half. He did it again, and again, until only tiny pieces fluttering in the kicking winds remained. And when he opened his palms he threw the shreds into the air, letting the wet whirlwinds carry them off across the treetops. She exhaled shakily, the hand on her chin feeling so strong; so divine. And he needn't say another word; trancelike and wanting she rose to her feet, her legs wobbling and rubbery; but she felt strength fill her anew when their lips met again, the fire sparked fresh; the desire renewed.

"I had to away to Emerys to ensure that you never signed it," he said, their noses touching; their hearts beating together, their souls afire. "Because I don't want a loveless marriage. I don't want convenience, I don't want any of that - what I want, what I've wanted since that night we sat together, since the night we made one another smile - is you. It's all I've wanted, Nadia. And if you tell me that I can't have that, that I've ruined that with my stubbornness, with my self-loathing, with my dedication to failing, then I will leave here and never speak with you again. But I will never forget you, or the time we shared, or the love that I let die in my heart."

"I don't want to let that feeling go. Since I saw you, I knew you were different," she admitted tearfully, grasping onto his waist with all her strength, her spine shivering as the leaves whipped up around them. "I've wanted freedom my whole life, but it's only with you I've learned freedom doesn't preclude the touch... the love, of a man," she admitted with a shudder. "In fact, I... I think... it's only with you at my side... I'd ever truly feel free." Their lips met again with all the passion and power in the world; not even in their most passionate moment together had they known this sort of full and freed desire. He swept her into his strong arms, holding her close and warm against the batter of the breeze; and as a cloak of red-orange autumn leaves swirled around them, their lips embraced and their bodies surrendered and they became one another. A sound of soft sobbing interrupted them, their kiss breaking as they looked to roadside to see old James, his suit muddied and lopsided, crying his eyes out at the sight of the two of them embraced and exchanging words of passion.

"She's broken that spell you've been under for so long," James sobbed, the old man's face ruddy. "Ms. Cauthfield and I've wanted nothing more than your happiness for so long, m'lord. To hear those words come from your lips, and to hear them so lovingly reciprocated, from someone so deserving of your affection..." he blubbered. "I can scarcely contain the joy, m'lord."

"James, has Ms. Cauthfield left our service yet?" Marshall asked pensively.

"Oh, come now, m'lord, you know that old witch couldn't ever leave us," James said with a dismissive wave of his hand. "Try as you might, m'lord, you'll never be rid of the two of us. She'd never have it, and she certainly will be brimming in pride to take credit for having forced you to confront yourself and realize you needed to make right with Lady Havenshire."

"I'm certain she'll badger me until the end of times about that," Lord Beckham sighed wistfully. His arm slung around his love, he looked down to Nadia, who herself had begun to cry streams of joy.

"I've never truly felt freer, Marshall, than you've helped me be," she admitted.

"Unfortunately, we've some more detritus to attend to, haven't we," Marshall grinned; a single bandit remained knotted down on the side of the road, groaning in pain. Lord Beckham approached the lawless cretin, hoisting him to his feet; as he dragged the man to the carriage, Nadia followed along with an impish smile.

"You've been practicing your fighting and shooting techniques, I would assume," Lady Havenshire teased, "...have you perhaps been practicing your riding techniques, as well?"

"M'lady, Ms. Cauthfield often enjoyed reminding me that love and relationships are about a great many things, one of which is sacrifice and giving to your lover," Lord Beckham responded facetiously, tossing the groaning criminal into the carriage and slamming the door shut, sealing it by placing his rifle across the latches to the door. "Unfortunately, there's one sacrifice I won't make - even for a woman as amazing and as beautiful, as talented and intelligent, and as free as you," he teased.

"Come now, m'lord, was Pierre certainly that difficult a horse to get along with?" Lady Havenshire laughed. "I could teach you, you know. It's not quite too difficult a task. Particularly, I would imagine, for a man capable of trouncing an entire half-dozen bandits with only a long stick to help him."

"A half a dozen bandits couldn't dare stand up to the stubbornness of old Pierre," Lord Beckham grumbled. "I think I'll be riding at the head of the carriage instead. James?" The loyal butler mounted the front bench of the carriage, still wiping tears from his eyes; her smile absolutely infectious, Lady Havenshire hopped upon Shadow's back, sighing in satisfaction as her steed clopped to life excitedly.

"Are we making our way back to the Emerys estate, m'lord?" Nadia asked excitedly.

"No, unfortunately - I feel we have a few stops to make first," Lord Beckham responded.

"Where to, then, m'lord?" James asked, so full of pride at seeing his master broken from the stupor that had afflicted him for so long.

"Well, I'm certain the local sheriff would have quite an earful for these criminals we're hauling, don't you think James?" Lord Beckham asked.

"I think he'd have quite a few things to say to them, indeed," James agreed.

"To the sheriff's then?" Lady Havenshire asked.

"And I think a second stop off - at the church? It's quite lovely for weddings this time of year," Lord Beckham added with a grin. A crack of lightning flashed and thunder followed - the sound of rain striking distant leaves filled the air, and a conspiratorial smirk covered Nadia's face quick.

"I'll race you there," Lady Havenshire responded happily.

"I'm certain you'll win," Marshall quipped.

"As long as we have love, Marshall, we both win," Nadia said.

EPILOGUE

"My love," Lord Beckham said, voice full of concern. He tended to the fire in the Berrewithe Manor study; its warmth radiated out calmly, blanketing the refuge of knowledge, books lined along the walls, a familiar couch set opposite the roaring flames - the couch from the gamekeeper's cabin, the couch he had spent his first intimate moments with Lady Havenshire upon. After Lord Havenshire passed, Nadia had the cabin demolished - but she could never part with that couch, or the memories of it, and had it carried forthwith to the Berrewithe estate, where she could appreciate it lovingly forever.

"Is something troubling you, Marshall?" Nadia queried, tilting her head in his direction as she lay upon the couch, enjoying the flicker and crackle of the dried-out logs set aflame.

"A great many things trouble me, love, though not necessarily all at once. I miss your father," he recalled painfully as he sat next to her, the old couch creaking beneath them. Reflexively he reached for his lover's stomach, rubbing it gently - he felt the roundness, the firmness beginning to show.

"I miss him, too, my love... but he'd be overjoyed to know soon he'll have a grandchild to carry on the family name... perhaps, if it's a boy, we could even name him for my father," Nadia added, smiling. "...that certainly can't be the only thought troubling you."

"I thought, the other day, on words you shared to me, before we married... of how our marriage, you thought, was meant to relieve my guilt over my... my sister," Marshall admitted painfully. "Perhaps it bore some measure of truth... that is, before I fell in love with you, perhaps, I hoped I could... do a little good, for this world. But I don't know. I don't know if I'll ever live a life worth earning my sister's forgiveness," Lord Beckham lamented, watching the flames of the fireplace leap and lick as his dearest love curled up next to him.

"When I said those things, I didn't quite mean them - or, I did, but I had the wrong ideas about you, m'lord. About your past," she soothed him. "I don't think I'm simply... a tool for you, not anymore."

"No, of course not, but... there's some truth to your words, nonetheless. I've overcome so much from the past, with your help, love," Marshall breathed deeply, that contemplative brooding taking him again, his expression deep and stormy; the way Nadia remembered it being that first night they met. "I broke from hating myself - something I very well may have done for the very rest of my days, if you hadn't come to help me. And for that I can never express anything except endless gratitude."

"I love you, Marshall - of course I wanted to help you find joy, and break the cycle you'd found yourself in," she confided. "Do you feel you haven't gotten past the... terrible things that happened to your sister, because of this world we live in?"

"I just... I miss her, Nadia," Marshall said, sighing deeply. "I've set so much right about this world and this life I live, but... Leah is still somewhere, hurting; hating our family, our name, because of what happened to her. I don't know that that can ever be fixed. If I can ever do anything to earn her love again." A quiet knock on the door interrupted Lord Beckham's introspection; he lofted a brow as loyal James entered the study, speaking in a hushed tone.

"M'lord, I beg your pardon for the interruption, but... well, someone has come to see you..." Lord Beckham looked to Nadia, whose smile brimmed bright and wide.

"Who is it, James?" Lord Beckham asked.

"I think that's something you ought to see for yourself," James grinned, giving a coy wink to Lady Beckham.

"What manner of plot have you concocted between the two of you?" Marshall questioned harshly.

"You expressed angst over whether or not you'll ever have made up to your sister for what happened, hadn't you?" Nadia asked.

"Well... y-yes," Lord Beckham responded, dumbfounded.

"I've spent my time alone sending letters... asking questions to friends of mine, of ours. Looking for names, sending more letters, and..." Nadia reclined on the couch, yawning. "...if you want to know whether your sister has forgiven you, or if she still loves you... perhaps you should ask her yourself." Marshall's eyes widened.

"Wh... what?" Confused, the duke raced down through the hall, down the stairs, and into the foyer, where the doors sat open, light pouring through. The duke at first thought her a dream; a sight he had never expected to see again. Dressed quaintly, in a simple white gown with a blue apron atop it, her blonde hair long and shimmering in the sunlight. Marshall collected himself as best he could; he'd recognize that woman anywhere.

"Hello, Marshall," Leah said, her face bearing a warm smile. "I've missed you."

"Leah," he said, his voice cracking with joy. "...I've missed you too, sister. So much."

"I heard I'll soon be an aunt?" Leah asked embracing her brother, whose eyes filled with tears of joy.

"Yes, Leah, soon," he answered.

"I can't wait."

Printed in Great Britain
by Amazon